Changeling Press. LLC

ChangelingPress.com

Samson/Lawdawg Duet
A Bones MC Romance
Marteeka Karland

Samson/Lawdawg Duet
A Bones MC Romance
Marteeka Karland

ISBN: 978-1-60521-851-9

Publisher:
Changeling Press LLC
315 N. Centre St.
Martinsburg, WV 25404
ChangelingPress.com

Printed in the U.S.A.

Editor: Katriena Knights
Cover Artist: Marteeka Karland

The individual stories in this anthology have been previously released in E-Book format.

Table of Contents

Samson (Black Reign MC 6)
Marteeka Karland

Charlotte: When I get into trouble, I go big. There was so much pain and fear, I turned my thoughts inward. To Samson. He's my knight in shining armor. The one man I've ever felt a real connection to. Then he was there, killing those who hurt me and sweeping me up in his embrace of warmth and safety. But now he sees me as a victim. Not a woman. It's up to me to prove I'm made of sterner stuff.

Samson: I had no intention of having sex with the little spitfire, but one look at Charlotte and I knew she was trouble. Our night was the kind of explosive a man can't walk away from, but I tried. Right up until her daddy showed up telling me she was missing and the last person she was seen with was one of the prospects from Black Reign. Wrangler, the little asshole, had her squirreled away somewhere and I knew if I didn't find her soon, I might never see her again.

Saving Charlotte from Wrangler will be a piece of cake -- after this his days are numbered. Which leaves me with time. Too much time. Time Charlotte's dad will have to convince her to leave me and come back home. So, how do I fight off another man determined to take my woman from me when that man is her daddy?

Chapter One

Charlotte

I huddled naked, shivering in the cold damp of the cinderblock basement I'd been thrown into. I had no idea how long I'd been here, but I was estimating at least two weeks. My body hurt all over. The chill made it worse. Also, it had been days since they'd brought me anything to eat or drink, and my stomach was gnawing in protest. Being in a damp basement had its advantages, though. I'd found a source of dripping water to drink. It didn't smell bad and wasn't discolored, but, honestly, I didn't have much choice. It was either drink the water or die. I suspected they were trying to starve me into submission. I could have told them it wouldn't work. I might be too weak to fight them much, but I'd fight to the very end.

There was thumping above me, and I tried to catch a glimpse of the men holding me prisoner through the cracks in the floor and the one grate that looked straight up into the house. Sometimes they would taunt me through that grate. I tried to use it to my advantage. So far, I knew there were at least five different men around this house who were there frequently. There were others, but they were mostly in and out. I suspected drug deals. Any time someone came down to try to rape me, it was always one or more of the five. So far, I'd been more trouble than a fuck was worth, and they'd left me battered and bruised. I suspected their patience was getting thinner.

Yelling followed the thumping. It sounded like there was a fight going on. I couldn't hear much of what was being said because they were too far away from the grate or in an area where there were cracks in the wood flooring.

A gun went off, booming throughout the house. I tried to hold back my whimpers, not wanting to draw attention to myself, but it was hard. Not only was I terrified, but I was shivering from the cold.

When the basement door banged open and a body tumbled down the stairs, I couldn't help my little shriek of terror. Immediately, I moved, getting between two free-standing shelves. They didn't have anything on them, but if I crouched down, I was pretty sure the shadows would hide me. Cobwebs blanketed my skin, making me cringe, but honestly, any spiders crawling on me weren't as bad as the men coming down the stairs.

Strangely, there was no dialogue between the two, just grunts and the sound of a fist hitting flesh as one man was beaten violently and the other one went about the grim task in silence.

The one doing the beating was a monster of a man. Huge. Hulking. I couldn't see much with the only light coming from the open door at the top of the stairs, but he wasn't someone who'd been here before.

"Where is she," he rasped out. His voice was deadly in its softness... and somehow familiar. I wanted to hope. To hang on to the possibility this man had come to rescue me, not to hurt me. Because if he decided he was taking me, there was nothing I could do to stop him. And he could probably kill me by accident with his hulking size. He almost reminded me of...

"Dunno, man." The man slurred his words. "'Spos't ta be don'eer som'mers."

"Charlotte!" the man yelled.

"Easy, Samson. If she's down here, you'll scare the fuck outta her!"

"S-Samson?" I whispered his name, but he must

have heard me, because he whipped his head around in my direction.

"Toss me a fuckin' flashlight," he barked. I heard him catch it, then a bright beam of light shone around the basement for a few seconds before landing on me huddled in my hiding spot. I winced and held up my hand to block the light I knew would eventually hit my face.

"Charlotte," he said, his voice softer now. "I need you to come out for me. Can you do that? I'm here. No one's gonna hurt you now."

I inched my way back out of my hiding place, the concrete floor scraping my bare hands and knees. I moved out of the little space slowly. When I stood, I was still crouched, ready to duck away from him if needed. "Samson?" My voice was scratchy from lack of water and from screaming so much over the weeks behind me. "Is it really you?"

Instantly, the light found me. I couldn't stop the whimpers or prevent myself from turning away from the bright light. Then the light was muted. A quick glance told me he'd turned it to point at the ceiling. Heavy footfalls approached me and, again, I whimpered, stepping back in reflex. My hand found something smooth and cylindrically shaped -- a pipe? -- and I grabbed it, surprised when it moved.

"Toss me a blanket," Samson said. He was right in front of me now. Much as I wanted to, there was no way I could look at him. I was so ashamed. This man... I'd dreamt night after night of him swooping in and rescuing me. I'd built him up in my mind to be my knight in shining armor. But now, I just wanted the man who'd made love to me over and over again during our one night together. He wasn't the white-knight type. In fact, after this, there was no way he'd ever see me as anything but a victim.

And what if this was all my imagination? What if it wasn't Samson here after all? What if it was a starved, dehydration-induced hallucination?

With as much of a battle cry as I could muster, I swung the pipe as hard as I could at the monstrous figure approaching me. I put everything I had left into that one swing. The sound of the pipe slapping against flesh was sickening in the dark. I had no idea what part of him I'd hit, but I'd definitely hit something. Then the pipe was yanked out of my hand with a grunt, and I nearly fell to my knees in despair. This was it. I had nothing left. They were going to take me.

* * *

Samson
Three weeks earlier

"What do you know about this kid, Rycks?" I didn't like prospects. Not unless I'd known them for a long damned time. Rycks was more forgiving. Not much, but he at least had some empathy.

"Wrangler's been prospecting for Salvation's Bane for a couple of years. Every time he comes up for a vote to a fully patched member, he's voted down. Always a holdout."

"He know who the holdout is?"

Rycks shrugged. "He figures it's Beast, the Enforcer. Seems Wrangler's brother had a hand in a situation Beast's woman found herself in when Beast met her. His brother has been 'missing'" -- Rycks made air quotes --"ever since. Wrangler says his brother got what he deserved, but he thinks Beast is holding a grudge."

"Can't say I blame Beast. Might not be right, but a man should feel at home in his own club. They tell him to look to us?"

"No. I'll have to contact Thorn, if you approve his request. I don't anticipate a problem, though."

I looked to El Diablo. The man had changed since finding his woman over Christmas. He was softer in some ways, but there was also a deadly edge that was even sharper than before. The other man and I stared at each other for a long time. A silent communication. Yeah. He had the same feeling I did.

"Talk to Thorn," El Diablo said. "I want all the background there is on this Wrangler and his brother. Everything. Then I want a face-to-face with the boy. Tell him I want to know everything about the situation his brother was in and exactly how much he knew. We'll hold him here at the compound until we receive everything from Thorn. If Wrangler holds back one piece of information or lies to me in any way, he's out. If the omission is egregious enough, he may be meeting up with his brother sooner than he'd like."

"I can live with that," I said.

With a nod, Rycks said, "Consider it done. I'll contact Thorn immediately. When do you want to meet with Wrangler?"

"The second he receives your message. If he can't be here immediately, tell him not to bother. Have Shotgun ping the GPS on his phone. I want to know where he's coming from and how long it takes him to get here. I also want to know if he makes any calls or texts, and who they go to."

Yeah. El Diablo had definitely changed. He'd always been cautious about letting men in, but he'd also taken a paternal role to any prospects we'd taken on, the same as he had the rest of us in the club. But now, he was even more protective of the women in the compound, and that meant he was more suspicious of any man he didn't know.

Waiting was not my strong suit. I'd hoped the little fucker would say he was out of town or in the middle of something important, but no. He just had to hop on his bike and haul ass to the compound as fast as he could. Got here in less than thirty minutes. I disliked him on sight.

He walked into the courtyard from the parking lot with a confident air. Kind of like he thought he'd soon own the place. His name was Jeff Allen. Also known as Wrangler. Somehow, he managed to show the required respect without really showing deference. Kid was good.

"I appreciate you giving me the opportunity to speak with you," he said, addressing El Diablo. "Most clubs probably wouldn't."

El Diablo just gave him a hard look. When he said nothing, I picked up the questioning.

"Thorn know you're here?"

Wrangler shrugged. "I told him I wanted to find a place I fit in. Told him I was asking Black Reign for the chance to prove my worth. He doesn't know I'm actually here because I was told to stop what I was doing and get here now if I wanted to discuss this."

Rycks raised an eyebrow, but El Diablo looked unimpressed. I continued.

"Give me one good reason why I should let you in here when a club with men we greatly respect won't let you go further."

"I don't have one. All I can tell you is that I'm a hard worker. I pull my weight. I'll learn anything you want me to so you can place me where I'll do the most good." He spread his arms out wide. "I just want a chance. I haven't done anything wrong that the patched members of Salvation's Bane have told me, but there's always a holdout when they bring my patch up for a vote. I'm sure it's Beast, and I can't say I blame him. My brother put his woman in harm's way. More than that, he betrayed the club and put them at risk. But I'm not my brother."

It all sounded very rehearsed.

He looked sincere. Sounded sincere. But something was just that little bit off. My instinct was to deny him, but I could tell El Diablo had other plans.

"Fine," he said. "You can prospect for us." That was El Diablo's way. He wasn't saying all he was thinking, though. "Rycks, set him up with a room. Once you figure out his strengths, see to it he has whatever training he needs to do whatever you need him to." Of course, that would likely take a while. More than enough time for Bane to get us the information we wanted. Then the real questions would begin. This was to be able to keep an eye on the kid until it was time to decide his fate.

I thought El Diablo was done, but then he stepped into Wrangler's personal space, his muscular frame and tall stature dwarfing the slighter, shorter young man. "You get one chance, Jeff. You blow it, or, more importantly, betray our club in any way, you're out. You do the latter, you die." Wrangler held his ground, but not before he swallowed, and a bead of sweat trickled down his temple. He nodded his understanding. "I need words, Jeff," El Diablo said, making sure there were no misunderstandings.

"I understand, sir."

El Diablo didn't move for long, long moments, then he eased back a step and gave his signature grin. "Well, then." He clapped his hands as if eager to get started. "Rycks, take care of matters as you see fit. Let me know if anything changes."

"On it, boss," Rycks said. He looked at me, and I could tell even he had his doubts. Rycks was usually known for picking up strays. Usually women who'd been given a sorry hand in life. Occasionally, he'd pick up a boy or young man. Like Wrangler here. But even he wasn't feeling it. The boy would probably never make anything but a prospect, but we'd see what he had. If he betrayed us in any way, he'd die. That simple.

A few days, I realized Rycks had put Wrangler in a position to be with Wrath. He'd given the boy permission to enroll in Palm Beach State College to be a paralegal. He'd have to work closely with Wrath to even make it through school. If Wrangler was on the up and up, he'd do well. If not, Wrath would be there to mitigate the damage. Seemed like a win-win situation.

Right up until the third girl disappeared from the same campus.

Chapter Two

Charlotte

Coming from a small town like Moore Haven, I loved getting to move to the city for school. It gave me the opportunity to do anything I wanted, as well as have some independence from a very overprotective father. Dad was the sheriff, and to say my dating life was nil would be an understatement. I didn't really care. All the boys I'd grown up with were lame. Palm Beach State offered a variety of flesh and blood, so to speak. I wasn't really concerned with boys. Sure, it'd be fun to get to go out and have fun, maybe experiment with sex, but I wanted to get through school and start a career so I could support myself. Much as I loved my father, I didn't want to go back to living with him.

It wasn't until my second semester that I met someone who made me rethink the whole study-hard method of college. And that someone wasn't who I first thought it would be.

Statistics was probably my least favorite course this semester and, two weeks in, I was already overwhelmed. The test the next day would be brutal. I knew that because the professor teaching it had a reputation of weeding out the students not committed to the class the first few classes. This test, given so quickly, would be one I either held a B or a C, or I fail. Then, I'd either have to drop the class, or spend the rest of the semester digging myself out of the hole. For this reason, my only plans this afternoon and evening were to hole up in my studio apartment and study.

Study, study, study.

With a bunch of capital letters.

But the school was having a bonfire on the quad.

I'd made several friends, and all of them were going. The responsible thing would be to go home and study. But hadn't I left my small town to live a little?

"Come on, Lottie, it'll be fun! You can leave early and still get in a few good hours of study before bed."

"You're killing me, Drea. You know I can't afford to fail this test."

"You won't!" she said emphatically. "You're the smartest girl I know. Ain't saying you'll ace it -- no one aces Mr. Christoph's first test -- but you won't fail it."

"Glad one of us has confidence in me," I muttered.

Drea and Susan each looped an arm through mine. "It'll be fine," Susan said. "Just a couple of hours. Besides, there's someone I want you to meet."

"Oh?" I wasn't really interested. I was too stressed out. But I didn't want to hurt her feelings.

"Yes!" she said excitedly. "I met him in Public Speaking. He's a natural and has promised to tutor me." She leaned in close so both Drea and I could hear without her being overly loud. "And the man is sex in ink on a Harley!" She grinned wickedly. "You've got to meet him. He's twenty-five and definitely *not* the boyfriend type, but he just screams 'hot ride.'" Both girls giggled. I found myself grinning with them.

"Fine. I'll meet your guy. *Maybe* I'll stay for an hour at the bonfire. But that's it."

Susan squealed and hugged me fiercely. "We're going to have such a good time! Our first college party!"

Drea laughed. "Which is pretty sad considering we've already been here a full semester."

"Come on. He's just over here." Susan grabbed my hand and practically dragged me to the parking lot. There, beside her car, was a guy leaning casually against a motorcycle. He wore dark jeans, a dark T-shirt, and a leather vest. When he turned slightly to throw up a hand in greeting to someone on the other side of the lot, I saw the vest had the word "Prospect" patched near the bottom in an arch curving upward.

"What does Prospect mean?" I asked Susan quietly.

She shrugged. "Something to do with his club. I don't know."

As we got closer, I could see there were tattoos scrawled over one arm, but they didn't seem to work together. Like they were a bunch of different images just jammed together. Interesting in its own way, but not like I was used to seeing in a sleeve tattoo.

"Wrangler!" Susan called, waving her hand excitedly.

The man's lips quirked up at the corners as he took in the three of us before settling on me. A shiver of pleasure went through me. Yeah. he was a hot guy, and he appeared to like what he saw when he looked at me.

"Well, hello, Susan," he said, his eyes still taking me in from top to bottom. "Who's your friend there?"

"This is Lottie," she said, using my abbreviated name. "I talked her into going to the bonfire with us tonight, so you better show her a good time. She wants to ditch us all to go study." Susan wrinkled her delicate nose as if the mere idea was distasteful.

"Is that so?" he said, standing lazily and stalking toward us. His tall, lean frame was at once intimidating and sexy. Not over the top, but he just gave off this bad-boy vibe that was catnip to college panties everywhere. "I guess I have my work cut out for me if I'm to tempt a beautiful woman away from her studies." His grin was devastating, and I'm sure he knew it.

"Well," Susan said, pushing me toward Wrangler, encouraging me to engage with him. "Me and Drea need to get ready. See you two at the party!" And just like that, my friends abandoned me with a blind date. I sighed. Should have known there was more to this than them wanting me to go to a party with them. They were trying to fill the void in my sex life. Which kind of took the fun out of the whole meetup. I sighed.

When they were gone, Wrangler grinned at me. "I guess we're on our own. We could get something to eat if you like? I know a great place just outside the city. We can get a great burger and chat." For the first time, he seemed... sinister. Though he was handsome, and I was sure could show me a really good time, I found I didn't really want to be alone with him.

"I appreciate the offer, but I really do need to study. I'll be at the bonfire but only for an hour."

"Wait. Are you tellin' me no?"

I blinked. "Um... yeah. I'm telling you no."

He shook his head, scowling. "Unbelievable."

"What's unbelievable?"

"You," he bit out, advancing on me. "Little tease. Leadin' me to think you were interested in hookin' up, then bailin' for no good reason."

"I told you. I have to study. I have Mr. Christoph for statistics, and I'd rather not have to spend the rest of the semester digging myself out of a hole."

He snorted. "Fuckin' cunt," he spat. "I'll show you what happens to little fuckin' cunts like you." He advanced on me and would have grabbed me. I backed up a couple steps just as the roar of another motorcycle sounded in the area.

My heart sped up. Was I being set up for rape?

Just as I was about to turn and run for my life, Wrangler backed off, throwing me a warning look. Another biker pulled in beside Wrangler's bike. He turned it off and sat there, staring at Wrangler with a hard gaze.

"Hey, Samson," Wrangler said, crossing the distance and holding out his fist, apparently for a bump. Samson just glanced at Wrangler's fist, then back to me.

He gave me a steady appraisal, then asked, "You good?"

I nodded, not sure what to say. If I told him Wrangler made me uncomfortable or was berating me, it could go bad for me. Still could, but I didn't get the threatening vibe I got from Wrangler. At least, not threatening toward me.

Samson nodded, then turned back to Wrangler. "Don't you got someplace you're supposed to be? Somethin' you're supposed to be doin'?"

Wrangler shot me an angry look. Like it was my fault he'd gotten in trouble. "Yeah. Was just on my way when the girl stopped me." He smirked, then added. "Some bitches have trouble takin' no for an answer."

I gasped, then kept my mouth firmly closed. Contradicting him would be the worst possible thing I could do. Sure enough, Wrangler shot me a venomous glance before getting on his bike. When he started it up, he revved it several times, making the pipes bellow. Then he sped off, peeling out as he went.

When Wrangler was gone, Samson turned his gaze back on me, looking his fill before he spoke. "What's your name, girl?"

I didn't hesitate. It was instinctual on my part. Like there was a person alive who could disobey this man. He had a look about him that said anyone who did disobey him was in for a world of hurt.

"Charlotte. Everyone calls me Lottie."

He was silent again for a long moment, his gaze holding mine until I had to duck my head. "Charlotte," he finally said. "Stay away from Wrangler. He's trouble."

Before I could stop myself, I asked him, "Are you trouble, too?"

He barked a laugh. "Honey, you have no idea."

When he didn't start up his bike, I gave him a curious look. He was still looking at me. Hard. Like he was trying to make up his mind about something.

"What?" I asked.

Samson shook his head slightly, breaking eye contact with me. "Where's your ride?"

I shrugged. "I walk. It's not far, and I need the exercise."

"Not a smart idea, you know. Woman alone in the city."

"It is what it is, I guess," I said. "I just have better things to spend money on than an Uber or a taxi."

"Yeah. Don't take an Uber." He sighed, turning his head away from me and shaking it slightly several times. It looked like he was having some kind of argument with himself. And losing. "Fuck," he said with another shake of his head. "Get on," he said. "I'll take you home."

"What's different about riding with a guy I don't know on a motorcycle versus riding with a guy I don't know in an Uber? Seems like the first option is more dangerous than the second."

"'Cause this guy you don't know ain't out to hurt you. Now get the fuck on."

Yeah. Probably should argue, but I didn't want

to. I was thrilled! Not only did I get to ride a motorcycle, but I got to do it with quite possibly the sexiest man I'd ever met.

Samson was probably in his late thirties or early forties. He was bald, but had a neatly trimmed beard and intense, silver-blue eyes. He wore a sleeveless black T-shirt that showed off heavily muscled arms I was sure would feel like heaven wrapped around me. As I got on the bike behind him, he grabbed one of my arms by the wrist and pulled it around his body. Yep. His abdomen was as rock hard as those glorious arms were.

"Where's your home?" I gave him the address, and he nodded once. "Hang on."

We took off smoothly. Soon, we were cruising down the road the mile and a half to my tiny apartment. Once there, I hadn't nearly had my fill of groping his hard body. Which was kinda twisted, but I was good with it.

He turned off the bike, putting the kickstand down but making no move to get off. He steadied me as I climbed off the back, careful not to touch the pipes and burn my bare leg.

"Thanks for the lift," I said, grasping at something to say to prolong my time with him. He hadn't spoken much, but I wanted to get to know this guy. It was like the intimacy of riding behind him was more telling than an hour-long conversation. While I was sure I'd enjoy the conversation, I found I wanted the physical stimuli more. I knew I was taking an offer of help and turning it into something it wasn't, but I was sure he felt something for me. Maybe it was my youth he liked, or maybe I was just his type. But this man was interested in me. It was only for sex, but I could see it when he looked at me.

He grunted but said nothing else.

"You want to come up for a cup of coffee?" Did I even have coffee in the apartment? No clue. I might be embarrassed if he said yes.

"No," he clipped, but he didn't start his bike. Samson didn't strike me as the indecisive type.

"A beer, then."

He raised an eyebrow. "Are you even old enough to drink beer?"

I shrugged. "I'll be twenty-one in a couple of months. If I happen to acquire a six-pack a little bit early, what does it matter?"

Again, he grunted.

Then something caught his eye. I wasn't sure what it was, but his gaze hardened and followed something behind me. I turned and saw a man walking down the sidewalk in front of my building. He wasn't paying us any attention and kept going, but Samson seemed to have taken his presence as a threat.

"Fine," he said. "I'll walk you up."

"I'll be fine, you know. This is a pretty safe neighborhood. The studio apartment I rent is overpriced, but I figure it's because the area is pretty secure."

"You can't be too careful," he quipped. "Come on. Besides, maybe I want that beer after all."

When he took my arm and gently urged me forward, my heart sped up. Was this really happening? God, I hoped so! I wasn't a virgin, but I knew I'd only scratched the surface of sex and pleasure. Could this guy do it for me? I was sure as shit turned on enough for him to. But would he?

"Know that look, girl," he said gruffly as we walked up the three flights to my tiny apartment. "You're too young for what I want."

I raised an eyebrow. "How do you know until you try?"

"Oh, I know." He waited until I opened the door, then followed me inside muttering, "I'm so fucked."

Once inside, Samson took up my tiny apartment. I'd forgotten about leaving the sofa bed out in anticipation of spreading my study material all around me. It was how I worked. Thank God I'd at least made the bed, so it didn't look slept in. That would be too much of an invitation to not be embarrassed.

"Sorry about the mess," I said, waving my hand to the bed. "I spread out my study material around me and go until I'm done." I gave him a sheepish look as I started to fold it back into the couch.

"Leave it," he said, then nodded to the fridge.

"Oh!" I hurried over and pulled out a Bud Light and handed it to him. "Hope that's OK."

He opened the can and took a couple gulps, never looking away from me.

"You don't talk much, do you?" I tried to flirt, but I knew I was doing a horrible job.

Again, he nodded to the fridge. "You gonna get one?"

"What? No! I don't drink much." Awkward much?

Samson turned the beer up and downed it, then sighed as he tossed the empty can into the box with the rest for recycling. "Come here, girl."

I swallowed but went to him. He reached for me with one hand and pulled me into his arms before covering my lips with his.

Right away, I knew this was going to be different. The second Samson touched his lips to mine, my whole body tingled. I gasped, and he deftly slipped his tongue into my mouth to tangle with my own. A startled whimper escaped me, and I just... surrendered. I didn't even try to take what I wanted or let him know what I liked or any of the other things I'd read or heard women did during great sex. I just let him have me.

He grunted, pulling me closer to him and lifting me, urging my legs around his waist as he carried me. I found myself on my small bed, Samson on his knees with my legs over his thighs as he stripped off that tight, black shirt. I did my best to wiggle out of my own shirt but couldn't seem to make my fingers work on the buttons. Above me, while he undid his jeans, Samson chuckled.

"Just relax," he said. "I'm more than capable of getting you naked."

"Thank God one of us is," I said, trying to make light of my nervousness.

Samson easily slipped the buttons through the little buttonholes and saved my shirt when I was ready to just rip it off. He also made short work of my bra and was working my shorts down my legs when he said, "I won't do more than you can take. Trust me, and I swear I'll take care of you."

I nodded. "OK," I said breathlessly.

"Good." He settled back on the bed after removing his boots, socks, and pants. Again, I had my thighs over his, but my pussy was now on vivid display. From the way he looked at me, licking his lips and staring at me, Samson liked what he saw. "Fuck me," he muttered, wiping his hand over his mouth.

Next thing I knew, his face was buried between my legs, his tongue doing wicked things that made me come unglued. I cried out, bucking against him from the foreign sensation, unable to stop myself. His beard abraded the inside of my thighs erotically as he continued his carnal assault. I wasn't a virgin, but oral sex wasn't something I'd had much of. There was no way I'd ever have sex without it again.

I was aware of Samson talking to me, but my ears roared so that I couldn't understand. Didn't try to. I just wanted to feel. It seemed like he took me right to the brink of orgasm, then let me fall back intentionally. At first I thought he might not realize how close I was. After the third time, when he chuckled at my frustrated cry? Yeah. He knew exactly what he was doing to me.

"Patience, little bird," he murmured against my heated flesh. "We've got all night. I told you I'd take care of you, and I will. The longer you give me, the better it will be."

I wanted to scream at him that, no, that wasn't a good plan, but I couldn't form the words. I was barely coherent, and we hadn't even fucked yet. He'd been right when he implied I couldn't handle him. At this point, I'd let him do anything to me he wanted as long as it involved me coming hard and soon. The first I knew would happen. I was terrified the "soon" wasn't in the cards. He'd hold out until he made me lose my mind. Maybe that was his plan.

Then he flicked his tongue over my clit. And kept flicking it while the pressure inside me built and built until all I could do was blindly reach for his head, holding him to me as I gasped when I came harder than I'd ever known possible. I couldn't even scream, the rush of pleasure hit me so hard.

The next thing I knew, Samson was lowering his weight on top of me. I felt him probe my entrance with his cock and realized that, somehow, he'd managed to put on a condom before sliding inside me.

I felt full. Stretched so that I burned. I must have

tensed up because Samson immediately kissed me again. He was gentle, coaxing my response as I whimpered into his mouth.

"Just relax for me again. I promise you'll adjust. And I won't take you hard until you're ready." He kissed me again, skimming his way down my neck to lightly nip at my collarbone. One hand found my breast and plucked at my nipple. His beard created an erotic tickling sensation over my skin where he grazed it, and I didn't know if was pleasant or uncomfortable. Maybe a combination of both? God! I didn't know!

My whimpers seemed to fuel his movements. I clung to his shoulders and wrapped my legs around his waist. Now, I wanted him to move, and digging my heels into his ass was the only way I could seem to tell him what I needed. Words abandoned me, because he'd rendered me speechless.

"That's it," he praised, kissing my lips. My cheek. My temple. "I think you're ready to be fucked. Aren't you?"

"S-Samson," I gasped.

"That's right, baby. By the time we're done here, you'll always remember my name. You're going to *scream* it!" His voice was rough next to my ear. That wicked sound was like a third hand to stroke my body to a fever pitch. "Fuckin' tight little cunt," he purred. "I can feel your heart pounding around me."

He started moving. Faster and faster until he found the rhythm he wanted. My clit throbbed with every stroke over it, my body on fire with need. Each stroke was that much closer to oblivion. I felt like there was a great chasm I was about to fall into, and I only wanted to careen faster toward it. Somehow, in the back of my mind, I knew this was a colossally bad idea. Not because of the risk of pregnancy or disease -- the guy was gloved, and I had an IUD. Because I would never be able to replicate this experience. Not even close. Already I'd experienced more pleasure than I thought was possible. And I was clinging to him like he was my lifeline.

"Come for me," he whispered in my ear, the devil on my shoulder. "Come on my cock and take me with you, Lottie."

For some reason, his use of my nickname was the trigger that pushed me over the edge. This time, I did scream, biting down on his shoulder when I did. He didn't seem to mind any pain I caused him, because I felt him swell inside me as my orgasm overtook me.

Then the only thing I could register was pleasure. My whole body seized. I couldn't breathe. Couldn't speak. When I finally sucked in a breath, I arched my back and screamed as I came and came.

Samson lifted himself off me, sitting back on his heels. He gripped the tops of my thighs and pounded into me, the veins on his arms and neck standing out in his exertion. He snarled as he fucked me, going faster and harder until, finally, his head fell back on his shoulders and he roared his release. I could feel his cock throbbing inside me as he filled the condom with cum.

Sweat coated both of us in a fine sheen, our breathing hard and gasping. All I could do was lie there and look up at him in awe. The defined muscles over his chest, abdomen, and arms made him look like a god. His full but trimmed beard contrasted with his bald head, giving him a bit of a sinister mien. In other words, the man was sexy as fuck.

For long moments neither of us moved. My arms were over my head while his hands stroked my thighs from hip to knee over and over. His cock was still deep inside me with no sign of softening.

Then Samson lowered himself slowly to me, finding my lips with his and kissing me tenderly for long, long moments. Slowly, he pulled out of me before getting to his feet and padding to the bathroom. It was the only other door in the place other than the exit, so it was no problem to find. He was there a short time before returning with a wet cloth. Surprisingly, he cleaned me gently before returning the cloth to the bathroom.

When he returned, he went to the kitchen and found a glass, filled it with water from the fridge, then brought it to me, sitting on the bed next to me. I took it gratefully and drank.

"You good?"

"Yeah," I said on a breath. "I... Thank you."

When I finished with the water, he took it and sat it on the table next to the couch/bed. He urged me to lie back down, and he pulled me against him. I was stiff at first, not knowing what to do. I'd never cuddled before. My few experiences with sex told me men didn't like to cuddle afterward. At least, not after just a hookup.

"Lie here for a few minutes," Samson said, kissing my temple. "I'll leave in a bit so you can study. But I want another round or two with you before I go."

I giggled. "Who said anything about studying? I don't need to study."

He chuckled. "Nevertheless, you're going to. At least, I'm not going to keep you all night. School is important."

"So's sex."

"Yeah," he agreed, the amusement evident in his voce. "So's sex."

He had his arms around me, and I lay with my

head on his chest, my hand resting on his shoulder. I wanted to snuggle into him, to breathe in his masculine scent of clean sweat, gasoline, and sex, but I was afraid to move. I didn't want to upset the mood and have him leave.

His fingers traced a path over my arm in a lazy slide, his heartbeat a steady, lulling rhythm at my ear. With the euphoria of the intense orgasms wearing off and the warmth of Samson's body next to me, lethargy overtook me, and I drifted off into a sleep filled with erotic dreams.

Chapter Three

"You've got to be fucking kidding me. Kidnapping? Are you serious?" That bad feeling I'd had about that prick, Wrangler, from the very beginning was growing. Fast. I was pretty sure the bastard was going to have to be put down at some point. With what Wrath was telling me now, it seemed like it would be sooner rather than later.

"It's circumstantial, but eight different witnesses put him with all three girls from Palm Beach State right before they went missing. It was enough for him to be arrested. The judge will let him out on bail until a formal indictment's made, but it looks pretty damning. He'll need Black Reign help to make that bail, too, because it won't be a small sum."

"Fuck," I swore. "Just Goddamn."

"There's more," Wrath said. From the sound of his voice, I wasn't going to like this next bit any better than I had the first. "I have one Sheriff Grady Bassett from Glades County requesting a meet with Black Reign." Definitely not something I wanted to hear.

"Why?" I barked the question. Any interaction with the law -- unless it was through Wrath -- was too much interaction in my opinion.

"Because his daughter is one of the missing girls. He said her friends mentioned her having met with Wrangler a few days before she disappeared. He'd been spouting off how he was a member of an MC and, of course, he threw Black Reign's name out there."

"Mother fuck," I growled. "Safest place for the pissant right now is in jail. He comes back here now, I may kill him."

"This guy means business, Samson. He's called in every favor ever owed to him to get Wrangler charged and in jail. He's not going to let this go. Right now, he's trying to get a warrant to have our compound searched."

"He must have some pull with someone if he can do that with a case not in his jurisdiction."

"Yeah. The guy is well-connected. Some through legal means, others through dirty cops and questionable tactics. He stays just enough on the legit side for me not to be able to say he's dirty himself. He's not afraid to bend the rules, but he's smart about it. Chooses his battles. This is a battle he's fully vested in."

I thought a moment. Normally, I'd need to discuss it with El Diablo, but I wanted this done quickly. The sooner we could nip the good sheriff in the bud, the better. Besides, I understood his anxiety. I'd think less of the man if he wasn't pulling out all the stops for his daughter. "Set up a meet. Do it there. At the DA's office. I'm taking full responsibility for this one and will discuss it with El Diablo later."

"Well, the fucker's here. If you can make the drive now, it would definitely be a good time. Not to mention it would get him off my back and onto yours." Wrath sounded only half amused.

"Good. Tell him I'll be there in thirty minutes. Got a name on his daughter?"

"Yeah. Charlotte Bassett. Goes by Lottie most of the time."

I froze. Charlotte? *Lottie!*

"Samson?" I must have been silent too long.

"Did you say… Lottie?"

"Yeah. You know her?"

How much did I want to admit to him? How

much could I admit to her father without getting my fucking throat slit? "Met her once. Three weeks ago. How long's she been missing?"

"Went missing a little over two weeks ago. Anyone see you with her?"

"Don't know." My mind whirled with what I needed to do. How to proceed. "Tell the sheriff to give me forty-five minutes. I'm going to have to have a brief discussion with El Diablo after all. Won't take long. Then I'll be there."

"And Wrangler?"

"Make his bail. I'll send Mechanic to come get him in a cage, but not until after this meeting. Wrangler and I have some shit to discuss."

"I'll set it all up."

"See you in forty-five." I disconnected the call.

Goddamned mother fuck! Lottie -- *my Lottie* -- was missing. I'd done my best to put her out of my mind, but I went to sleep thinking about her at night and woke up with my first thought being to wonder what she was doing. And if she'd found a man. All this time I'd been worried about Wrangler trying to get her to take up with him, and she'd been missing. So help me God, if Wrangler'd harmed one hair on her beautiful head, I'd kill the little motherfucker. Fuck. I'd likely kill him anyway. If he had anything at all to do with her disappearance -- and it looked strongly like he did -- he was a dead man walking. For more than one reason, but mostly because he'd hurt Lottie.

I found El Diablo's number in my phone and waited until he picked up.

"We got a problem," I said, cutting to the chase.

"Wrangler. Yes. We need to know if he's responsible for the missing girls." I would never understand how the fucker knew things as fast as he did. It seemed to be worse now that Loki had joined us. The man was eerie in a way I couldn't describe. He was nice enough, but I always had the feeling he saw more than anyone other than El Diablo himself.

"There's more. I was with one of the missing girls three or four days before she went missing. Her daddy is the sheriff of Glades County, and he is singularly determined to find her. No matter who he runs over to do it."

"Understandable. Has he put Wrangler together with Black Reign?"

"Yes. Wrangler ran his mouth at the college. He's definitely tossed the name Black Reign around more than he should."

"Well, I know you have a plan, or you wouldn't be calling me," El Diablo said. That normally clipped English accent was drawling now. I liked that he had that kind of faith in me.

"I've set up a meet with him through Wrath to take place at the DA's office. I'll feel the man out. See what his agenda is beyond getting his daughter back. Wrath says he lives on the fringe."

"So not a goodie two-shoes, but not dirty either."

"Exactly. I have a feeling the man will insist on doing his own investigation into Black Reign. My hope is to keep it to him. Not his team or his department or whatever. Only him."

"Good. Get Shotgun all the information on him you can. See if he can dig up some dirt."

"Wrath said Wrangler will be out on bail. I'm having Mechanic transport him to the compound. Once he's here, if he has anything to do with this fuckin' mess, I'll get it out of him."

"We'll all help you, Samson. He's a threat to all of us."

"Do we really want to expose the whole club to this? I can take care of it myself with maybe one other person as backup. Then if anything happens, I'm the only one exposed."

"Not happening. You keep me informed. I want to know the second that meeting is over."

"Understood."

I did, too. El Diablo was going to make a point. Wrangler was going to regret crossing him and this club. I had no idea why Wrangler chose Black Reign to gain entrance when he clearly had a foot deep in Salvation's Bane, but I was certainly going to find out. Right after I took care of the sheriff.

The ride was uneventful but gave me time to think. I should have been thinking about what all I needed to say to Sheriff Bassett. Instead I was thinking about Charlotte. If she was hurt, I was gonna cut up Wrangler into little pieces and feed him to the gators. The more I thought about Charlotte the angrier I got. The more desperate I got. She'd been gone for more than two weeks. Another day was too fucking long.

The second I walked into the conference room where Wrath had the good sheriff, I knew this was going to be unpleasant. Sheriff Bassett's gaze fastened on me, his eyes hard and cold. The man was as determined as I was, and he was gauging me. Given his time in law enforcement, I had no doubt he could see beyond the shields I normally had firmly in place and knew this was personal.

I sat at the spot Wrath indicated, directly across from Bassett. Wrath introduced us, but neither of us blinked.

"Gentlemen," Wrath said with a soft warning in his voice. "We can accomplish more together than we can as adversaries."

Bassett glanced at him with annoyance. "We *are* adversaries. His club has a member who knows where my daughter is. I'm not foolish enough to think they're not getting ready to bail him out of jail right now. Probably while I'm pussyfootin' around with this asshole." He indicated me.

"I assure you, we have the same goal," I said softly.

"You think so?" Bassett gave me a hard look. "See, let me tell you what I think. I think you'll do anything to deflect blame from your club. So pardon the fuck outta me if I don't believe you'll work too hard to see if your boy's responsible. In fact, I believe the only thing you're doing is hindering the investigation. So, yeah. I want a look inside that compound of yours."

"Wrangler will be dealt with," I said softly. "Much more harshly than the justice system could. If he's responsible -- or even knew what was going on -- he's going to suffer everything she suffers twice over." I gave Bassett my own death stare. "Just so you know. Black Reign is my family. Wrangler isn't a patched member, so he's not fully one of the family. Had he been, he'd know the world of hurt he's brought down on himself if he's guilty."

"Oh, yeah? How do you propose to find out? Ask the motherfucker?"

"Exactly that." I shrugged. "With a few enhanced interrogation techniques. Trust me when I tell you, if Wrangler knows where Charlotte's at, I'll get it out of him."

Bassett narrowed his eyes. "I want to be there."

I held the man's gaze for long, long moments. Normally, this wasn't something I'd even consider. I was going to do all kinds of things outside the law, but

I got the feeling this guy wouldn't balk. I didn't trust him, but also knew he was the type of man to do anything to save his daughter.

"Sheriff Bassett, I'm going to lay this out for you so you know where I stand." I knew Wrath was going to have a shit fit later, but this had to be done or the sheriff would be a major obstacle in finding Charlotte. Not because he would try to interfere, but because we didn't have time to follow the rules of law. She'd already been gone far too long.

To my surprise, Wrath picked up the thread I was starting. "Your daughter's been gone over two weeks. Any investigation my office starts will be well past a recoverable phase. Forty-eight hours is pretty much the limit, ideally. Statistically, the longer she's gone, the less likely she is to be recovered alive."

"You think I don't know that?" Bassett snapped. "It's why I'm here in the first place. Trying to cut corners."

"You're welcome to help with this," I said. "But you have to understand we'll be doing this our way."

"And we have no intention of prosecuting those involved," Wrath finished.

There was a heavy silence while Bassett processed this. I could tell the moment he understood what we meant. He nodded slowly. "So, we do what we have to and... what? Let everyone go?" He knew that wasn't part of the agenda, but he was feeling us out.

"No," I said. "We take care of them. That gonna be a problem for a lawman like you?"

"Not at all," he said without hesitation. "But when we find whoever is responsible -- be it that little weasel, Wrangler, or someone else -- I want him."

I nodded. "Yours to deal with as you please.

Black Reign will help with the aftermath so there is no mistake. Everything stays off the books. You use as many of your own resources as you're comfortable with, but there will be no official investigation."

"Got no problem with any of that. I just want my daughter safe."

I stood then, offering my hand to Bassett. The other man got to his feet and accepted my hand. His grip was firm, his gaze steady. I was looking at a man determined to do whatever it took to get his daughter back. I could only speculate what he saw when he looked at me. Because I knew without a doubt I would kill whoever it took to find Charlotte. Because, somewhere inside me I didn't want to acknowledge even to myself, I knew she was mine.

Mechanic was waiting with a truck to take Wrangler back to Black Reign. Shadow and Tank had come with Mechanic to ensure there were no problems. We'd lucked out on getting Shadow. The man had originally come from Bones in Kentucky but had migrated south with one of Bones's members -- Stunner. And, of course, El Diablo knew him. After that he and Fury had hit it off, and he'd agreed to stay. Shadow would definitely be an asset in this case. He was huge and a powerful fighter. The intimidation factor was strong with this one.

Wrangler seemed oblivious to the trouble he was in. Likely he thought he could spin some song and dance and could talk his way out of it. I escorted him out of the detention center. Fucker was chatty as hell.

"Motherfuckers'll learn to mess with Black Reign," he said with a chuckle, like this was all some big misunderstanding or, worse, a slight against the club by the police. "Can't wait to see the looks on their faces when Wrath gets me off completely. That'll be some happy crappy right there."

I clenched my jaw to keep from replying. And my fists to keep from throwing the bastard a beat-down right there. As we approached the truck, Wrangler gave a jolly wave to the ride. He couldn't see the men inside because of the tint, but he still didn't suspect he was in trouble.

"Mechanic brought a ride just for me? I've got my Hog, you know. It's in the impound, but when you guys get it out I can ride home myself."

"Get in the fuckin' truck," I said, not looking at the bastard. Instead, I busied myself with firing off a text to El Diablo that we were on his way and to have a tarp down in the common room. I had a feeling there was going to be blood when we got there, and I didn't want to ruin the wood floor.

"But I need my ride --"

"I said, get in the fuckin' truck. Ain't sayin' it again, motherfucker."

He glanced at me but shrugged. "Fine by me. Just don't forget my bike. It was expensive." It was a piece of shit, but I refrained from commenting.

Wrangler opened the front passenger's door to find Tank sitting there. Instead of telling Wrangler to get in the back, however, Tank got out and shut the door. He opened the back door and indicated Wrangler should get in. Shadow sat on the driver's side back seat, looking mean and intimidating as ever. Wrangler got in, but when he went to shut the door, Tank simply climbed in after him, forcing the younger man to move over to the center seat. Tank nodded briskly at me, then shut the door, and they took off. The look on Wrangler's face as the door shut made me smile. The first real satisfying feeling I'd had since I'd heard about the mess with Charlotte. If nothing else, I'd get the pleasure of beating the fuck out of the little weasel.

The trip back to the compound took twenty minutes. We wasted no time. Sheriff Bassett followed. Four more Reign members met us halfway out and fell into line, one in front of the sheriff, two behind. If Bassett felt cramped, fuck him. This was for his protection as well as our own. I'd been in the lead, but Loki was the fourth member of that convoy, and he took the lead, leaving me free to think about this upcoming interrogation.

By the time we'd pulled around to the garage and stowed the vehicles, I was ready to do this. Sheriff Bassett's vehicle -- which was his private truck, not the official county vehicle -- was parked alongside the rest of us in the garage where we could control when he left. The other man didn't balk or look resentful. Instead, he looked grimly determined and eager for the next phase. We hadn't spelled it out exactly at the DA's office, but he had to know this wasn't going to be pleasant. None of it was. And there was no intention of a single motherfucker responsible for this kidnapping ring getting out of it alive. Or ever being seen again, really.

Mechanic and the others sat in the truck awaiting my instructions. Glancing at my phone, I saw there had been a few texts from Shadow. Apparently, Wrangler still didn't appreciate the amount of trouble he was in.

Shadow: *Fucker's bitching about being mistreated by the cops and about his bike. Says they beat it up, and he'll probably need a new one. Shit's expecting Reign to foot that bill too.*

Thank God for auto complete. Shadow was notorious for shorthand texting, and I could never decipher what he meant. This I got.

Me: *Keep him there until I say. I want to clear the*

common room of non-essentials and make sure it's prepared for a messy interrogation.

Shadow: *Copy that.*

The common room was deadly silent. We normally had better places for this, but doing it in public served two purposes. First, it kept the sheriff in check. He could only see what we allowed, and he wouldn't see anything more damning than the discipline of one of our own. Second, it served as a warning for anyone in our house who thought to betray us in any way. Unsanctioned kidnappings and human trafficking were a sure-fire way to betray us. Everyone knew we weren't all warm and fuzzy. But we didn't harm innocents.

The ol' ladies weren't present except for Fury's woman, Noelle, and El Diablo's woman, Jezebelle. Noelle had taken her role as Fury's woman seriously. In some ways, she was more suited to violence than Fury. He was a doctor and took that title -- and his oath -- proudly. He had trouble with keeping someone alive so we could tear him down further. Noelle helped soothe those anxieties for him. In fact, I was pretty sure she'd take it over for him if she could. She was a fighter. Not a doctor. Her mental strength was hard as diamond when it came to the suffering of someone who deserved it. Fury always saw the human underneath. As expected, Noelle stood slightly in front of Fury, to his utter annoyance. Several times while I surveyed the room and the preparations made for this interrogation I saw him move her, but she stubbornly refused to hide behind him. It was clear she intended to take the brunt of the event and give him a place to turn his head when he wanted to call a halt.

"Is the boy ready?" El Diablo asked. Jezebelle stood beside him, her face an expressionless mask. I hadn't expected her to be here, but she was the president's ol' lady through and through. She'd stand with her man even if he didn't want her to, and not even The Devil could stop her.

I snorted. "He's either terminally stupid or believes he's got one over on us."

"Which makes him terminally stupid," El Diablo drawled. "Well. That's soon to change. He motioned to the chair we had readied. It was bolted to a wide, square platform and resembled an old-style electric chair. I could strap him in with leather restraints if I wanted. In fact, I might just do that. It would definitely get the point across before the first blow was delivered. "Are you doing this, or will you give me the honor?"

I glanced at him. "You're the prez."

"Yes, but it's your woman who's in danger."

That caught me off guard. "Never said she was my woman."

He squeezed my shoulder. "You didn't have to."

Well... shit. Maybe she was my woman. I hadn't really thought about it, but I'd broken every rule I'd ever set for myself when I took her that night. She was way too young for me and had forever written all over her. That and she was the most passionate woman I'd ever had the pleasure of fucking.

No. Fucking wasn't the word for it. She'd taken me to a whole new level of pleasure. I'd been able to take what I wanted and still make her scream with desire and beg me for more. I remember lying there with her after she'd passed out from all the times I'd made her come, thinking I'd never had the pleasure of aftercare with a woman. Not like this. Holding her after sex had been a high no drug had ever given me. When I'd left her that night, I'd done so reluctantly and with her sound asleep so she couldn't talk me into staying. Because I would have.

So, yeah. Maybe Charlotte was my woman. Her daddy was gonna just love that.

When the convoy got back to Black Reign, Wrangler wasn't thrilled about being there. At least, not in the manner in which he was brought. Or the sight that greeted him.

"What the fuck, Samson?" Wrangler protested when he was escorted into the common room. "What's all this?"

"This," Rycks said, stepping in front of me before I started on the little fuck before it was time, "is an interrogation. Yours." He motioned to the seat in the center of the dais. "Take a seat."

"Is this some kind of joke?" He scoffed. "I'm the one wronged here. I was arrested for no good reason and accused of shit I didn't do."

I didn't have to restrain myself this time. Rycks backhanded him for me. Wrangler spun around and stumbled backward before tripping over his feet and falling to the floor. Rycks was on him almost instantly.

"You're a Goddamned liar!" he bit out. "You know where the missing girls are, and you're going to tell us. How much of you is left to dispose of when this is done depends entirely on the information you give us."

"It wasn't me!" he yelled back angrily, blotting his split lip with the back of his hand. "I don't even know what you're talkin' about!"

"You do," El Diablo said, his crisp English accent somehow decorating the brutality of what was about to happen. "And you'll tell Samson. Eventually. Personally, I'm hoping you hold out for a very long while. Samson is particularly eager to find these girls. If you cooperate, he might even let you live long enough to see them safely here."

"I don't care about no bitches gettin' back here! *I didn't do anything, you motherfuckers!* Go find whoever did it and ask them what the fuck's goin' on!"

El Diablo's face went hard. He looked like he wanted to kill the boy right there. Instead, he glanced at me and nodded.

"Strap him to the chair," I ordered. I didn't care who did it as long as someone did. Several of the patched members eagerly stepped forward to force Wrangler into the chair. He protested and threatened before starting to plead when they fastened restraints to his arms and legs, then his head. Just like an electric chair. "Now," I began. "You've earned the beating you're about to get for disrespecting the president just now. After that, we'll see how much more punishment you earn before you're allowed to die. It all depends on how readily you give me the information I want."

"So, I'm dead no matter what? How's that encouragin' me to help you?"

"Ask me that when I'm through with the first beatin' you've earned."

The next hour passed in silence from the club. Wrangler, however, screamed and begged. Until he couldn't. The canvas on the floor caught the splatters of blood, and the chair held firm on the dais, no matter how much he thrashed or how much I punished him. Both of his eyes were swollen shut, I was certain I'd broken at least a couple of ribs, and he was missing three toes on one foot.

"Give him a minute." The soft command came not from Fury, but from Noelle. Fury's expression was hard. He had his hands crossed over his chest and looked like he could give a fuck if I stopped or not. He nodded, agreeing with Noelle, so I backed off.

"Now," El Diablo said in a conversational tone. "Are you ready to tell us where the girls are?"

Wrangler whimpered, blood and spittle dripping from his mouth. He'd probably lost a few teeth as well.

"There's a house on the outskirts of the city," he said, his words slurred and barely recognizable. "A guy from the school told me he took girls there. I knew about it, but I've never been there."

"Calling bullshit on that," I said. "Not interested in your fuckin' excuses or tryin' to place blame on somebody else. I just want the location and directions."

"Please," he said, breathing heavily. Blood sprayed from his lips with his words. "You gotta believe me. This ain't my fault!"

"Then give me a name, and the team will look into him. But, you should know, if we find nothing, if you lie to me, I'll make sure you last *weeks* before I finally let you die."

He whimpered again. "I d-don't remember his name."

"Of course, you don't," Rycks said. "Location! And you better not fuckin' lie, motherfucker."

When the boy balked again, trying to pretend he had no clue what we were talking about, Shadow stepped forward beside Rycks and me. I was a big man. Rycks was shorter but just as muscular. Shadow... was a hulking behemoth compared to the two of us. The big African American knelt down so he could be at eye level with Wrangler. The man, though his eyes were starting to swell, looked at Shadow like he was staring at the Devil himself. Shadow had that effect on people. He was overall a pretty laid-back guy, but in the right situation, he was one deadly motherfucker.

"You're gonna tell the nice men here what they

wanna know," he said softly. "If not, it'll be my turn to take you apart. You don't want that, son."

Wrangler's bladder let go as he whimpered.

Then he gave us a rough location. Shotgun fed the details into the computer from where he and Esther were working. They didn't need to be present for this and, quite frankly, Esther would never have been able to stomach it. She was too tenderhearted.

It wasn't long before the pair came up with a set of directions and set up a drone ready to get some intel. Mechanic and Razor loaded it up and headed out, hoping to get close enough to get good surveillance without getting close enough to tip off any occupants.

While we waited, Fury saw to the worst of Wrangler's wounds. It wasn't out of concern for the boy. He just knew it wasn't time for Wrangler to die yet.

"Close the compound," El Diablo ordered. "Club girls and prospects are confined to their rooms. Families should stay in their sections but are free to move around their assigned courtyard and the pool area unless Samson, Rycks, or I say otherwise."

It would be several hours before we had the information we needed on the location Wrangler had given us. Until then, there would be absolutely no chance of anyone betraying the club -- which was why the club girls and prospects were locked down -- or our families -- which was the reason for keeping them separated from everyone else. Families were sacred to Black Reign. For me, that now included Lottie, even though neither she nor her father knew it. Hell, I had no idea if I understood it. I'd only met her once. But the girl left a lasting impression on my heart. Welcome or not.

After Wrangler finally quit his whining, still strapped to the chair, half in, half out of consciousness, the wait began. No one spoke. Hell, hardly anyone moved. To a man, they all had their eyes on either Wrangler or El Diablo.

It was five hours later when Shotgun checked in.

"That's the place, Samson." Shotgun was normally quirky and fun-loving. He could make anything into a joke when the situation called for it. Now, he was deadly serious. "There's two girls in the house. Neither of them look like Charlotte, but the audio I'm picking up indicates there's probably another girl in the basement they won't let out."

"Whether or not she's there, that's our play. If we find her, we'll call it a win. If not, I'll come back here and beat this fuck some more." I was done playing. Wrangler was going to die a slow, painful death. If Lottie wasn't there, I was going to take him apart a piece at a time. I looked over at the little piss-ant. He could barely open one eye and had been in and out of it most of the last few hours, but now, he was focused on me. So I focused on him. "You better hope she's there. You better pray to whatever god you hold dear she's there and unharmed."

"Just kill me now," Wrangler said, his words slurring. "I'm sorry."

"You are sorry," I said. "But no. I'm not killin' you just yet. How easily you pass from this life to the next depends entirely on the shape Lottie's in when I find her."

The boy started crying, begging for his life in tiny whimpers. I glanced up at Fury and Noelle. Fury shook his head, not an ounce of compassion in his eyes. Noelle actually rolled her eyes and muttered, "Fucker could at least act like a man."

"Sheriff." I looked at Grady Bassett. The man was as hard as any of us. "You stayin' or goin'?"

"Not missing this," was all he said.

"You good with what's about to happen? No one's gonna be arrested. There will be no trials."

"Your boys'll clean it up?" The sheriff quirked an eyebrow.

"They will."

"I'll do anything, kill anyone, to make my daughter safe."

"Then you ride with us. Mechanic," I said, nodding to our Road Captain. "Bassett goes with you."

"You got it."

I looked to El Diablo. "We have your permission to roll?"

"Get the women out and to safety. Then kill anyone left."

I nodded. "Consider it done."

The trip took an hour. Then it took another hour to finalize our entry plan. The drone showed only eight men in or around the little cabin. I shuddered to think about what the basement was like in a tiny place like this. If it had concrete or cinder block, it would be damp and cold, likely filthy as well. If Lottie had been there for weeks, there was no telling what kind of condition I was going to find her in. I just hoped this was the right place. If she wasn't here...

"I have eyes on all eight men," Shotgun said from my earpiece. "Six outside. Two inside. The ones inside are... with the girls."

"Shadow, Iron, and Tank can take care of the outside maggots," I said. "I want Bassett with me. Loki, go where you can do the most good."

"I'll help with the outside scum," he said, his voice raspy. "It will be a clean death, which is more than they deserve. The ones on the inside can burn when we torch this place."

"You sure about that?" I didn't really care about how the men died, I just wanted to make sure any remains could be explained properly.

"It will look like a meth lab explosion," Loki said with a shrug. "People die in those all the fuckin' time."

I nodded. "OK, then. Rip it up, men. We get the girls out, then, once everyone is secure, we'll search the basement. I don't want any accidents."

Everyone nodded solemnly in agreement.

The fight was on.

Chapter Four

Samson

It took us less than half an hour to dispose of the men outside. They did it without so much as a sound, which meant the men inside with the women had no warning whatsoever.

We entered the house through the front and rear. Once inside, Bassett and I found the remaining men. Bassett, true to his word, dove in without heed for the safety of our targets. He pulled one guy off a girl he was raping and beat the fuck out of him with as much violence as Loki did with the other man.

"Keep at least one of those fuckers alive," I cautioned. "We need to find any other women they're holding."

"Oh, they'll both be alive for the grand finale," Loki said.

"Very much alive." Bassett squatted down in front of the man he'd subdued. He was sitting cross-legged, hands tied behind his back, looking up at Bassett with hate. "When this place goes up in flames, you'll be sitting here. Waiting to burn to death." Bassett's voice was husky. A deadly rasp. "I'm gonna stand out there and listen to you scream. Pleading for someone to end you. You'll beg before you die. Just like these girls begged." Then he stood and stepped back.

The guy sitting there spat at Bassett, sneering at the sheriff as if asking him what he was going to do about it. In a lightning-fast move, Bassett struck out, kicking the bastard in the face.

"That's police brutality!" the guy screamed. Which got the second person doing the same.

"What in this fuckin' world makes you think

we're the police?" Loki asked with a grin. "Do we look like fuckin' cops to you?"

"Well, technically," Bassett said, tilting his head to the side as he knelt back down in front of the second guy we'd restrained, "I guess it is police brutality. But guess what, motherfucker. No one gives a fuckin' shit about you."

"You'll never get away with this."

"Like you aren't getting away with what you did to these girls?" Bassett snorted. "One thing. We're smarter than you. And meth labs explode all the fuckin' time. Yeah. We'll get away with this, motherfucker. Now. Where's the other girl?"

"Fuck you!" The guy screamed.

I heard Bassett beating on the little fuck, but I searched around the small house, looking for the way into the basement.

"Guys," I said over the radio to the team outside. "Can you spot any way into the basement outside?"

Tank answered. "There's a stairway going down a level to a door, but it's barricaded. I'm sure it goes into the basement, but it will be difficult to get into. There's got to be another way in they access easily."

"Continuing to search the house," I said. "Start the cleanup outside."

"Already on it, brother," Mechanic said. "Figured it would be easier to put them all in the house when it blows. Several of them, but still completely believable. Besides, we found syringes and needles all over the fuckin' place out here."

"Sounds good. Bring 'em in."

The two girls had been evacuated. Iron took them out and would be back with the truck before we blew the place. For now, my only concern was finding Lottie and getting her the fuck outta this Godforsaken shithole.

"The house is fuckin' tiny, Samson," Tank said. "How many fuckin' places can they hide a door or a trap door or a grate or some shit?"

"Yeah, well..." I was searching one of the two bedrooms. It was filthy. The bed had only a dirty mattress with stains. Semen. Blood. Urine. The thought of Lottie in this place was abhorrent. The longer I searched without a sign of how to reach her, the more my chest constricted.

I was just about to tell Tank to bust down the door he'd found outside the house when I noticed grooves on the floor next to the dresser. There wasn't much showing. Like they hadn't gotten the dresser in the right place. I pushed. Behind the dresser was a door.

"I think I got it," I called. "Bassett. Loki."

"Boss?"

"Get me a flashlight. I think I've got it."

"On the way, boss."

"You get her outta there, Samson," Bassett said. "I'll be there as soon as we get all these fuckers inside." I heard flesh hitting flesh. "Where is she!" Bassett yelled at one of our two prisoners. He'd dragged the man into the room where I'd found the door.

"Where is she," I rasped out.

"Dunno, man." He slurred his words. "Spos't ta be don'eer som'mers."

"Charlotte!" I yelled.

"Easy, Samson. If she's down here, you'll scare the fuck outta her!" Loki was usually a calming influence, the few times I'd been around him.

I took a couple of deep breaths, trying to rein in my emotions. Killing these guys was too good for them. "They deserve to suffer," I muttered.

"Oh, they will, Samson," Loki said softly. "I swear to you, they will."

"S-Samson?" A soft whisper came from the dark below.

I turned my head but could see nothing. As I eased down the stairs, I called out to Loki. "Toss me a fuckin' flashlight." I caught it, then passed the bright beam of light around the basement for a few seconds before I landed on a small figure, huddling naked on the concrete floor between two metal shelves. She winced and held up her hand to block the light when it passed close to her face.

"Charlotte?" I tried to make my voice softer. Nonthreatening. "I need you to come out for me. Can you do that? I'm here. No one's gonna hurt you now."

She inched her way out of her hiding place, her hands and knees leaving bloody streaks where the concrete abraded her tender flesh. When she stood, she was still crouched, ready to duck away from me. Ready to hide.

"Samson?" Her voice was scratchy. "Is it really you?"

"Yeah, baby. It's me," I said, but she didn't seem to hear me. Her hands were moving around the shelves next to her, but I couldn't see what she was after. Probably just trying to balance herself.

She whimpered continually, holding one hand up to shield herself from the light. I immediately turned it up to shine on the ceiling. It gave me light to see by but didn't startle or blind her.

As I approached her, trying to soothe her, I called back to Loki. "Toss me a blanket." I was right in front of her. I could have pulled her into my arms, but I knew that would be the wrong move. I thought Lottie knew it was me here, but she still looked terrified, and she wouldn't look at me.

Just as I made a slow move to put the blanket around her shoulders, she let out a battle cry and took a swing at me with something I'd missed. I caught the cylinder in my hand with a slap and pulled it from her. A pipe of some sort. She let out a heartbreaking sound of despair as she fell to her knees.

"Lottie, honey, I'm not gonna hurt you."

"NO!" she wailed. "Oh, God, please no!"

"Charlotte." I put a firmness in my voice I hoped she'd respond to. "Look at me," I commanded.

Slowly, obviously not wanting to, she looked up at me. Her face was swollen, her body bruised. She shivered, probably with a combination of fear and cold.

"Do you see me, Charlotte? Tell me who you see."

She just shivered for several seconds, then took a breath. "S-Samson."

"That's right, baby. I'm here. You're safe. I'm not gonna let anyone hurt you ever again."

"Y-you're n-not with th-those o-other m-men?" My heart nearly broke right there.

"No, baby. I'm here to kill every one of those motherfuckers." I had no idea why I said that. Knowing I was going to kill would probably scare her more. If it did, her father was here. Maybe he could help. Instead of cowering back into her hiding space, she let out a ragged sob.

"Samson!" She cried my name, then lunged into my arms.

* * *

Charlotte

A soft, warm blanket fell over my shoulders and

was wrapped around my body. Then Samson lifted me into his arms. Another man took the flashlight from him and guided his way out of the basement and up the stairs. All the while, Samson kept telling me he was here. He was with me, and no one would ever hurt me again.

I wanted to cry. Wanted to scream at the injustice of it all, but I just lay passively in his arms. I couldn't even turn my face into his shoulder, not wanting to take any more comfort in him only to have it stripped away. I hurt all over, as much from the cold as from the beatings I'd taken. Thankfully, I didn't think they'd broken anything, but even Samson's gentle motions hurt me.

We reached a big, black SUV, motorcycles all around it. I spotted my father walking toward us. The sobs that had abated threatened to start up again, and I closed my eyes, finally deciding to take the refuge Samson offered with his big, wide chest. I turned my face into him and inhaled deeply. Strangely, his scent, the one I'd dreamt about both before and after my capture, calmed me. He was my rock. The one person I could count on. Much as I loved my dad, he was in sheriff mode, as I liked to call it. He was taking care of business in his own way. Apparently, without the help of his department, which meant they truly had killed the men in this house.

Dad approached and laid his hand gently on top of my head. "I need to take her to a hospital," he said softly. I stiffened in Samson's arms. I didn't want to go to a hospital. I wanted to stay with Samson.

"How you gonna explain her injuries?" Samson's voice rumbled in his chest. Again, it comforted me when I never thought it could. "Let me take her back to Reign. Fury's our doctor. He can look at her. If she needs anything he ain't got access to at the compound, he can get help without taking her someplace public."

There was a long silence. Dad stroked my hair, which made me cringe. I was so dirty... so fucking dirty...

"Fine," he said in a clipped tone. "I'll be there to take her home after this mess is cleaned to my satisfaction. I want nothing left that can link back to her or any of the other girls."

"Loki will escort you. Can you ride a bike?"

Dad snorted. "I can ride or drive anything with a motor."

"Good," Samson said. "You can bring my bike home."

"Well, that's surprising," my dad muttered. "Thought you biker types were protective over your bikes."

"We are," Samson said. "But Charlotte is more important than a fuckin' bike, and she needs someone familiar."

"Which leads me to so many questions I can't even begin to work them out. But now's not the time."

"See you at the compound."

Samson climbed in the back seat of that big SUV. Instead of buckling me into a seat, he sat me on his lap and kept his arms around me, tucking the blanket more securely around me and adding another one.

"We'll be home soon, little Lottie," he murmured. "We'll get you taken care of, and then you can rest."

I stayed quiet and still. There was a man driving and another one in the front, but I shut everyone out. Even Samson. All I concentrated on was his steady heartbeat under my ear. Somehow, my fists had curled into his shirt, and I clutched it tightly, not wanting to let go for any reason. With Samson and my dad there, I knew I was safe. But the thought of facing anyone right now was just too much. I just wanted a bath. No. A hot, hot shower. Where all the nasty filth could be washed down the drain and I could scour my skin with the heat.

We must have arrived at the compound Samson mentioned because the door to the SUV was opened, and he stepped out with me securely in his arms. He took me inside one room, then on into another one before laying me down on an exam table.

Immediately, another man started talking. "She hurt anywhere obvious?"

"She hasn't made a sound or winced since I picked her up. Where are the other girls?"

"Treated and resting. Once they're ready, they'll contact their families or go their own way. El Diablo has given them permission to stay as long as they like."

Then a woman was beside me. "Hey, Charlotte," she said with a kind smile. "I'm Noelle, Fury's woman." She stroked hair back from my face gently before laying an ice pack to the side that was swollen. "Fury's our doctor. I promise he'll be gentle, but we need you to talk to him. Can you do that?"

I glanced at the other man in the room. He looked scary as fuck, but like he would stand there an eternity if I didn't give him permission to examine me. Just… waiting patiently. Finally I nodded.

"Good," Noelle said. "That's good. Can I remove the blankets? I'll be careful to keep you covered. I promise." Again, I nodded.

Fury was careful, both not to touch me unnecessarily and not to expose me any more than strictly necessary. In the end, he took a few X-rays and put in an IV.

"Well, she's got nothing broken," Fury said. "Pretty dehydrated and bruised all to fuck."

"She been raped?"

Fury sighed. "She says no. I didn't do a pelvic exam. That would be too traumatic for her right now. But the bruising I saw didn't indicate it. I'm inclined to believe her. I don't think she's just trying to hide it or prevent me from doing an exam."

"So, physically..."

"She'll heal. Just give her a place to feel safe and secure. Her mind will take longer to heal than her body."

God. Didn't I know it.

Then Samson was pulling a chair up to sit beside me. He took my hand gently in both of his big ones. "Hey, there."

I looked at him, unable to do anything. Tears leaked from my eyes. I'd prayed for him to rescue me but hadn't thought about how he'd see me broken and helpless. It was a humiliation I wasn't certain I'd ever get over.

"Hey."

"You're safe now. You know that, right?"

"Is..." I swallowed. "Is Wrangler here?"

For some reason Samson didn't answer that question. When I tensed, he pulled my hand to his mouth and kissed my fingers. "Don't worry about Wrangler. I've got him taken care of."

"He's here. Isn't he?" My heart pounded, and I broke out in a sweat. "Oh, God!"

"Worry not, sweet Charlotte." Another man came just inside the room. He was dressed immaculately in a perfectly fitted suit. A woman was at his side with sympathy in her eyes but also fierce determination. Then another woman came in to stand by Noelle. "Wrangler is being dealt with. He won't hurt you or anyone else ever again."

"I'm Jezebelle," the woman said. "That's El Diablo, my man. He's the president of Black Reign. If he says something, you can bank on it."

Noelle spoke then. "I asked a couple of the girls to come be with us so you don't feel so outnumbered by the guys." She smiled gently at me. "Just please understand they will all protect you while you're here."

I nodded, though tears continued to leak from my eyes. I looked back at Samson, gripping his hand, not wanting him to let go. He seemed to understand, because he gave me a level look before nodding once, bringing my hand back to his mouth for another kiss.

"They're right, baby," Samson said softly. "Wrangler's being taken care of. You'll never see him again, and he'll never harm another soul."

I nodded again. What I wanted to say was that I wanted the motherfucker dead. But I didn't. Again, Samson seemed to see into my soul. He gave me a solemn look. "Don't worry. He's getting everything he deserves."

Again, I looked to Samson for confirmation. I couldn't seem to keep my eyes off him. He was my safe haven. The one I trusted to protect me when I had no reason to. Sure, Samson had rescued me, but he had no obligation. Shouldn't I be wanting my dad to take me home?

"Samson," I whispered.

"What is it, baby?"

"Will… will you stay with me?"

"Honey, I ain't goin' nowhere."

"Promise?"

"I'm with you as long as you want me to be,

honey. And I never, ever break a promise."

For long moments, I just tried to breathe. I gripped Samson's hand hard, not wanting to take any chances he would try to leave me alone.

"Where is she?" As if I'd summoned him, Dad walked into the room and stopped the second he saw me. There was a hard look in his eyes. His jaw clenched and unclenched. "Baby girl," he said, his voice hoarse. "I'm gonna take you home."

I whimpered but bit it back as much as I could. My grip on Samson's hand tightened. There was another girl with my father. Looked like she'd escorted him in here. She approached me now, looking at my and Samson's joined hands.

"Hey, sister," she said softly with a smile, reaching out to stroke my hair gently. I cringed because I was still dirty. I hadn't taken a shower yet, and I knew I was filthy. "I'm Eden. Samson's sister. Welcome to the family." Her smile was genuine.

"She's not part of your family," Dad said, moving close.

Eden turned and put herself between my dad and me. "She's part of this family if she wants to be."

"I need to take her home. Where she's safe."

Eden nodded. "I can understand that." I couldn't stifle my whimper, and my grip on Samson's hand tightened. The thought of going home should make me happy, but the thought of being away from Samson terrified me. He was my rescuer. He was the one who'd promised to keep me safe.

Eden turned when I made that little sound. Again, she stroked my hair and took my other hand. "You don't want to go with your dad? He seems pretty capable to me."

"I just..." I glanced up at my dad before closing

my eyes, ashamed that I didn't fully trust him to keep me safe. Tears streamed down my face. "Dad has to go out sometimes. He's the sheriff. He can't be with me all the time."

Eden whipped her head around to look at my dad. "Is that true? What did you plan on doing if you had to go out? Is her mom there? Who'd stay with her?"

Dad just stood up straighter, a blush high on his cheeks.

I looked at Dad, pleading silently with him to understand. "It's not that I don't want to be home, Dad. I just... Samson promised not to leave me. I'd feel better if I was with him."

"Baby," Dad said, taking a step forward. "You don't know these men."

"No, but I know Samson."

"You think you know him, but he's just as violent as the rest of them."

"Look, buddy," Eden said, taking a hostile step toward my father. "You might think you know who Black Reign is, but you don't. If Charlotte stays, that means she's part of this whole family. While she's here, they will protect her with their lives. Yeah, they're all rough and wouldn't hesitate to kill a motherfucker if they had to, but they are protective to a fault. What's theirs is defended to the death."

"Charlotte is not theirs," Dad said vehemently, taking a threatening step toward Eden. Fury and Noelle stepped between the two. "She's my daughter."

"Daddy," I whispered. "I need to stay here. I... I need it." Dad was right in that I didn't know these men. I didn't really know Samson. We'd spent one blessed night together. One. If he'd wanted to hurt me, he'd have done it then. Because Samson was a warrior.

I could see it on his face when he'd picked me up out of that basement. No way a warrior as strong as Samson took pleasure in hurting a wounded animal. He'd want a battle worthy of him. And, right now, that wasn't me.

"Back off my sister, Bassett," Samson said. "If Charlotte wants to stay here at Reign, she'll have all kinds of mean men just lookin' for a reason to kill someone. Having someone threaten Charlotte would give them the excuse they want. That includes me, if she's ever threatened by me. If she feels safer, what's the harm in giving her what she wants? It's not like you don't know where she's at or who has her."

"Besides," El Diablo said. "You wanted your shot at Wrangler. While my offer to take care of him still stands, you can't very well get the information you want from him and take care of your precious daughter at the same time." Apparently, this had been an ongoing conversation between my father and El Diablo.

Dad sighed. "Fine. Yeah, I need to finish this with that fucker. I'm convinced he knows more than he's letting on, and there are more women being held. I've been following this fucking gang for months." He scrubbed a hand over his face. "Never thought my own daughter'd be caught up in this."

"Good. You have the use of our interrogation room with Wrangler. There will always be two brothers with you in that room at all times. While I don't much care what you do to the boy, I want to know exactly what you do and what information you get." He smiled. "I'm just controlling that way."

"Your house," Dad said. "Your rules."

"Then it's settled," El Diablo said with a smile. "Little Lottie will stay with Samson here at Black Reign until you're finished with your investigation, or she's ready to leave."

Dad came over to me and bent to kiss my forehead. "You need me for anything, sweetheart, call me. I'll check in on you every day."

I nodded my head. "I love you, Daddy."

"I love you too, baby girl." He looked up at Samson with a hard stare. "I'll be back to get her when this is over."

"You can take her home when she's ready," Samson said, not backing down. "Not before."

I hated hurting my dad. For so long it had been just him and me. But this wasn't something he could make better. I wasn't certain anyone could. I just had to wonder how long Samson would try. A man only had so much patience.

Right?

Chapter Five

Samson

God as my witness, there was no way in fucking hell I was ever giving up Lottie. She needed me. And, by God, I wanted her. Once she was stronger, once she'd put all this behind her, she might want a younger man, but I had every intention of spoiling her so much, of making her feel so safe and protected, she'd never want to leave me.

I started the second Fury said she was ready to go. He'd given her two bags of fluids, cleaned her cuts and scrapes, and made sure she had something for pain. Eden rounded her up some clean clothes, and we took her to my rooms.

"Do you want me to help you shower?" Eden asked Charlotte. I had to bite my tongue to keep from denying her. If anyone was going to help Charlotte, it would be me. Unfortunately, that wasn't my decision to make. It had to be Charlotte's.

"No," Charlotte said softly. "Thank you, though."

"I programmed my number into your phone," Eden told her. "If you need me, all you have to do is text, or tell Samson."

Instead of answering, Charlotte just nodded. Eden gave me a look. "I'll see you later, then. Samson will keep you safe."

Again, Charlotte nodded. "I know."

With Eden gone, I was left alone with Charlotte. She sat in a chair, clutching the blanket around her, looking as dejected and miserable as anyone could. I walked over to her and scooped her out of the chair. She didn't protest, just laid her head against my shoulder passively. Taking her to the bathroom, I sat her on the toilet while I started the shower, heating the water.

"You want it hot or cool?"

"Hot," she said softly. "Hot as I can stand it."

"Thought as much," I said, gruffly. I was going to have to stay with her whether she wanted me there or not. Otherwise, I knew she'd burn herself trying to scrub clean. I wanted to punch something. I took out my phone and shot off a message to El Diablo.

Me: *I want the kill.*

El Diablo: *Not sure I can promise that. Her daddy has a valid claim as well.*

Me: *Negotiate.*

El Diablo: *I will.*

I adjusted the water while she sat there. Charlotte made no attempt to move or to take over her own care. She was probably overwhelmed and still in shock. "Come on, baby," I said. "You'll feel better once you're clean."

"Not sure I'll ever be clean again," she whispered. Then her head snapped up. "But I didn't let 'em rape me." She looked fierce as any warrior when she said this, shaking her head. "I didn't. I fought 'em."

"I know you did," I said. This was a delicate situation. I knew whatever happened in the next few minutes, the way I handled this situation, would set the tone of our relationship from here on out. "You were brave to fight. They could have killed you, Lottie."

She nodded her head. "They wanted to. When I fought, I hurt more than one of them, but they weren't as big as you."

"Ain't many people who are."

"When I saw you. Coming down those steps. When you got close to me..." She shuddered, pulling the blanket tighter around her. "I didn't give up. Exactly. But I knew there was no way I could fight you off."

"But you still would have." I made the statement firmly. Almost an order. "You did. With the pipe."

She nodded at me. "Yes. I would have fought until I died. If they'd managed to tie me up -- and they tried -- I'd have still fought." She looked up at me again, tears in her eyes. They weren't tears of sorrow or shame. They were of a fierce pride. "I'm not weak!"

"No, Charlotte. You're anything but weak." I took one slow step toward her. Her tears were killing me, but I knew I couldn't touch her unless she made the first move. "You're a strong, capable, fierce, brave woman. You'd never stop fighting."

"No. Not for myself. Not for my children."

"Not for your family."

"No. I'd never stop fighting for my family. Or my friends."

I nodded. "You know what that makes you, Charlotte?" When she shook her head and shrugged, I answered my own question. "That makes you the woman I want for my own."

She gasped, her eyes going wide. "Don't say that," she whispered. "Thoughts of you kept me sane. Kept me wanting to fight until you came for me."

"Then you admit you want to be mine?"

Those lovely, copper-colored eyes of Charlotte's held me captive as she took her time answering. The sheen of tears glistened in the metallic pools of her eyes, but she refused to let them fall. Her chin jutted out stubbornly but quivered slightly. "I've been yours since the night we made love. I knew I'd never find a man I wanted more than I wanted you. I never thought I'd see you again, but I knew it was only a matter of time before I sought you out." She swallowed. "When they took me, when I was thrown into that basement because I injured a couple of those bastards, I built a fantasy in my mind where you knew I was missing and refused to stop looking until you found me. Then you'd kill everyone in that motherfucking house and bring me home."

"Baby, that's exactly what I did."

"I know. So, if you want me, I'm yours. I'm scared. A little broken. But I'll never stop fighting as long as you're with me."

I couldn't stop myself. I pulled her into my arms, blanket and all, and hugged her to me as hard as I dared. Charlotte sobbed like her heart was breaking. Then she screamed in agony, clinging to me as hard as she could. Her grief was overwhelming her. Me, too. But I knew she needed to get this out. No way I was letting her do it on her own.

The bathroom filled with steam while she raged on. All the while she clutched me, not allowing space between us. I just let her cry, not trying to stem the flow of her tears or lessen her sobs. I held her just as tightly as she held me.

Finally, she began to sniffle more than sob. Then she asked me a question I found odd. "You won't let anyone take me from you. Will you?"

"Never. I protect what's mine."

She shook her head. "I don't mean the bad people."

Then I got it. "Baby, no one in this world will take you away from me unless you want to leave. Even then, I'm not sure I could let you go willingly."

"Dad may try --"

"No. He won't. If you want to leave, you can leave. Not sayin' I won't follow you. And I'd never keep him away from you. You're his daughter. Unless he hurts you physically or mentally, I'll never come between him and his daughter. But I won't let anyone, including your father, take you anywhere you don't want to go."

That seemed to satisfy her, because she nodded her head before stepping away from me and moving toward the shower. She dropped her blankets and stepped inside under the spray. Fury and Noelle had cleaned the worst of her wounds, but she still needed a shower. Her hair was lank and filthy, her body streaked with dirt. She ducked under the water. Rivulets of mud ran to the floor of the shower to be washed away down the drain. She looked back at me. "My arms and ribs hurt," she said matter-of-factly. "I could use some help with my hair."

"Baby, there's nothing more I want than to get in there with you, but I don't want to push you."

Lifting her chin, she snapped at me. "You sayin' I don't know what I want? I'm not asking you to fuck me, Samson. Just help with my fucking hair."

I had to bite back a smile. She was pissed, but her response was exactly what I would have expected from the woman of a biker. She was still hurting, still scared and still feeling like she'd never be clean again. This was a blatant challenge to my assertion I wanted her for my woman. Well. I was up to the challenge.

Shedding all my clothing except my boxer briefs, I stepped in with her and reached for the shampoo. A generous dollop in my palm later, I lathered her hair in slow strokes and squeezes of my hands. Carefully, I massaged her scalp, trying to pay attention to her body language. The last thing I wanted to do was hurt or frighten her.

Charlotte sighed, her body relaxing. When she

did, I used one soapy hand to gently pull her against my body so she could lean on me. She did, laying her head against my chest while I took the detachable sprayer and gently washed the soap from her hair before smoothing conditioner through it and rinsing it.

Once her hair was clean, I found the shower gel and rubbed it over her body in a light caress. She was so bruised I was afraid I'd hurt her, but she never made a sound. She just moved her body to assist me, turning to let me wash her front.

"Do you have a razor?" she asked softly. "I feel like a Sasquatch."

Nodding, I stepped out of the shower and got a clean one from a pack and snagged the shaving cream as well. "It ain't girly shave stuff, but it'll work."

She smiled. "It will."

"So you want me to leave now?" I asked, not because I wanted to leave, but because I wanted to make sure she still wanted me there.

"No," she said. "I'll need your help again in a minute."

I just nodded, watching raptly as she removed the body hair from under her arms and from her legs from ankle to high on her thigh. When she'd finished, she looked up at me, handing me the razor. Then she sat on the built-in bench in the wide shower stall, taking the shave cream and rubbing her hands together to create the necessary foam. Spreading her legs wide, she rubbed the cream carefully over her mound and the crease of her thighs.

"Shave me," she said softly.

"You sure?"

"I am."

Slowly, I got to my knees in front of her. I pushed her thighs as far apart as I could with no resistance from her. When I looked up at her, she nodded. So I began. With slow, careful strokes, I shaved her as completely as I could before bringing the spray between us to rinse the cream from her skin.

"Samson," she whispered. I could see the need in her eyes. I also knew she wouldn't ask for this after her earlier outburst.

"You're beautiful, Lottie," I said. If my voice was gruffer than usual, I'm sure it wasn't because there was a lump of emotion in my throat. This woman, who had been through so much, needed me. Maybe she needed to know she was beautiful and desired after all she'd been through. Maybe she just wanted to feel human again. Whatever her reasons, there was no way I was turning her away. I'd take things slow, but I was going to give her as much pleasure as I could, as gently as I could.

I dipped my head between her thighs to swipe my tongue from her opening to her clit. She gasped in a sharp breath, but arched her back, pushing her little pussy toward me.

"More," she breathed.

I licked and sucked her lips and all around, occasionally dragging my tongue over her clit until she cried out. Using my thumbs, I spread her lips open so I could get to her cunt, stabbing my tongue inside her to draw out her honey. She was wet and slick, and so very responsive. Just like before. Her hand landed gently on the top of my head as she ground herself against my mouth. I grunted in praise, thrusting two fingers inside her slowly, pumping them in and out. Her little clit quivered under my tongue with each stroke of my tongue, and her pussy pulsed around my fingers. "Can you come for me?" I rasped out, flicking her clit once before sucking it between my lips.

"I -- yes. Yes... Oh, God! Samson!" She let her head fall back against the shower wall and screamed, her body seizing as she pushed through the orgasm. The fine muscles of her abdomen undulated as she rode my face, prolonging her pleasure. I reached up her body with my free hand and gripped her breast firmly but gently, rolling her nipple with my fingers. Long seconds later, she gasped in a breath, her chest heaving as she panted for breath. "Samson..."

"Yeah, baby. You're so beautiful when you come." I petted her pussy, kissing it lightly, then each inner thigh. I stood, pulling her into my arms. She seemed more relaxed, but she still clung to me. Which was fucking fine by me. If I had my way, she'd be right by my side for the foreseeable future.

I shut down the shower, then kicked my boxers into a corner before drying us both. Stepping out of the enclosure into the bathroom, I reached for one of my T-shirts I'd brought for her and helped her into it.

"Is this yours?" she asked, wrapping one arm around her body and using the other hand to bring the neck of the shirt to her nose where she inhaled deeply, her eyes closing. I snagged a pair of lounge pants and put them on sans underwear.

"Yeah, it is. That OK with you?"

"It's like I have you wrapped all around me." Her voice was higher pitched than normal. She was probably checking out. Not aware of what she was saying.

"That's right. And that's where I'm gonna stay until you tell me to go. You get me?"

She nodded, inhaling again. I snagged a brush, then lifted her into my arms and took her to the bed. I sat at the head and pulled her between my legs and began the process of detangling her hair. It took a long time. At one point, I was afraid I was going to have to cut it, but, somehow, I managed to get it all smoothed out. The long, chestnut strands sifted through my fingers like silk. Charlotte sat with arms wrapped around her legs and her chin resting on her knees. She hadn't made a sound, and I thought she might have gone to sleep. But she hadn't.

"Thank you, Samson. For everything."

"There's nothing to thank me for."

"Yeah. There is. I know you killed people tonight. Then you brought me home with you, washed me, and brushed my hair until it's dry. I got the feeling before you weren't used to being gentle, but you did it. For me. So, yeah. Thanks. Both times."

I set the brush aside and urged her into the middle of the bed beside me. I helped her under the covers before pulling her small body against my much larger frame.

"The best thanks I could get is you letting me hold you like this. I wouldn't surprise me if you never wanted any man this close to you ever again."

"I don't," she said. "I only want you."

"Well, you've got me, Lottie. I'm yours, but you're mine, too."

"I can live with that," she said as she yawned. Then she was utterly still, her head pillowed on my arm, my arms solidly around her.

If anyone had told me, before I'd met Charlotte, that I'd be in this position, I'd have called them a Goddamn liar. I never wanted this kind of closeness with a woman. It had felt that way the other time with her as well. I wanted to wrap her up and keep her close. Keep her safe. I hadn't done either last time. This time, however, I'd walk through hell to keep her exactly where she was now.

Chapter Six

Charlotte

The next two weeks went by like a dream. Mostly, I stayed with Samson in his room. We played silly board and card games with each other or with Eden. Occasionally, some of his club would come over with their women -- ol' ladies -- and we'd have game night. Or movie night. I got the feeling Samson was trying to get me used to being with his club in case he had to be apart from me, but he never mentioned it.

I really liked the women. They were fun and warm. Never once did they mention my ordeal other than to ask how I was doing. Once. After that, they just banded around me, bringing me into their unique and exclusive club of biker women. If Samson ever took me out into the compound -- and the thing was like a university or a resort with a quad in the middle for outdoor meetings and parties -- the women always surrounded me with their friendship. There were a few women Eden called club girls who gave me venomous looks when Samson wasn't looking, but the others told me not to worry about them. They were just upset Samson was off the market.

One afternoon, Samson had to leave for club business. I thought it probably had something to do with Wrangler, but I didn't ask, and he didn't offer. Which left me with Eden and four guards. Shadow, apparently, wasn't a member of Black Reign, or of their sister club, Salvation's Bane, but of another club somewhere in Kentucky called Bones. He worked with several of the Salvation's Bane members and had made close friends with Black Reign. I wasn't sure, but I thought he and Fury might have a past, but it wasn't my business. Either way, he, Fury, Iron, and Tank were there to keep an eye on us. They didn't intrude or carry on conversations, they just took up a spot out of the way and watched our surroundings.

"What are they looking for?" I asked Eden as we lounged in the sun by the pool. Lyric and Celeste played in the water with their daughters, and I absently petted a giant dog lounging beside me.

"Who?"

"The men. They look like secret service agents." I waved my hand in the air, looking for a better description. "You know. With bite."

Eden laughed. "Yeah, I guess they do. To answer your question, they're just making sure things don't go sideways. We're perfectly safe inside the compound, but Samson doesn't take chances with his family. He's making extra sure. All you really need to worry about in here are club girls. They might pick a fight or something, but they're basically harmless."

"Are you sure? Some of them seem to really dislike me."

"Honey, they're just pissed about you and Samson. Club girls consider any unattached male theirs. Samson has attached himself to you, so he's now out of their reach."

"Wait. But I saw Iron with one of them the other day. I thought he was with you?"

She laughed. "Nah. We're just fuck buddies. I will hate to see him find his woman, but she ain't me." She glanced his way, giving him a little wave. His expression never changed from that hard "on guard" face as he gave her a two-finger salute and continued scanning the area.

"So… are you…?"

"A club girl? Yeah." She grinned. "But only because it makes Samson uncomfortable. I'm closer to your age than his. He practically raised me, so he tries to pretend to have a say in my life."

"You mean he doesn't?" I asked with a chuckle. "If he didn't, I'd say you'd have more than Iron after you. I mean, since you're just fuck buddies."

She smirked. "Who says I don't?" We both laughed.

Eden sighed happily. "I'm so glad Samson found you, Charlotte. You're the sister I always wanted and never had."

I smiled at her. "Thank you, Eden. That's one of the nicest things anyone's ever said to me."

"You keep my big brother in line. I don't want you leaving him."

"I doubt that will happen. Only…"

"He being an ass already?" She frowned.

"No! Not at all! He's so sweet and patient. I just… Well, he doesn't think I'm ready for sex. At least, not all the way." I hurried, wanting to get this out before Eden interrupted. "We've fooled around, and he always gives me orgasms, but he won't, you know, have sex with me." I looked away. "If I was less secure with myself and him, I'd be afraid he didn't want me after… you know."

"Oh, girl," she said in a sympathetic voice. Followed with, "I'm so disappointed in you!"

"Wait. What? Disappointed? I wasn't expecting that."

She laughed. "Honey, Samson's over-the-top protective. Always has been. He likely thinks you're still physically and emotionally fragile. Take the bull by the horns, so to speak." She shrugged.

"You mean, take matters into my own hands?"

"Exactly. He won't fuck you? Take the fuck to him."

I grinned. "I'm so glad we're friends. That's exactly what I'm gonna do."

"How are you feeling?" Eden asked. "I mean, do you still have nightmares?"

"I haven't had one in several nights. It helps that Samson is always with me at night."

"But how do you feel?"

I thought about that question. Really thought about it. I glanced at the building where I knew Samson was inside having his meeting with the club. "I can't say I'm not uncomfortable at the thought of leaving this compound, but if I had Samson with me, I could do it. I'm not looking over my shoulder constantly anymore. I even thought about going back to finish school, though I think it would be better if I could get online courses. I know I don't ever want to go back to that campus."

"Have you talked to your dad?"

"Yes. Every day. If I haven't called him before bedtime, he calls me. I think he's a little upset I won't come home, but I also think part of him knows I'm safer here than with him because he can't always be with me. Hell, I know he does or he'd insist I come home."

"He seems like a good dad." Eden gave me a glance but looked away from me when she spoke.

"He is. He's loving and protective, and he's the best dad in the world. It hit us both hard when Mom died. I know he's still grieving, but I wish he'd find someone. He's a really good guy and I don't want him to be alone." I sighed. "This is the longest stretch he's been without me home since she passed."

Eden shifted in her seat. "Well, one thing's for sure, he doesn't take someone hurting you lightly. From what I hear around the club, he's been with

Samson and El Diablo nearly every day since they brought Wrangler here. They go to the interrogation room and question him. Or something. Lyric told me Rycks even raised an eyebrow at how... insistent your dad was at getting the information he wanted. He's in the process of taking down a pretty big sex-trafficking ring, and it looks like Wrangler was at the center of it."

"Wow," I breathed. "If he hadn't taken me, this might have gone on for a long time. Lord! This club would have been in so much danger, to say nothing of all the girls they could have grabbed!"

"El Diablo is pretty on top of things. He'd have figured it out. But yes. That thought has been mentioned more than once. No one is glad you suffered, Lottie, but we're all glad they caught on to what Wrangler was doing."

"Believe me, I didn't want to go through it either. But it's a small price to pay for girls like Holly and Bella to be safe." I nodded to the two kids swimming with their mothers. "Because, if Wrangler had been able to continue, thinking he could get away with it, you better believe he'd have tried something."

"I don't want to even think about that," Eden whispered.

We sat in silence for a long while. Somehow, I'd come out of this with only a battered body and a few nightmares. My trust in strangers was probably toast, but I didn't need to worry about that just now. I watched as club members filed out of the building I'd been watching. Sure enough, the second Samson was out the door, I spotted him.

With a grin, I stood, putting on my shoes. They were bright yellow, four-inch heels to match my bikini. Grinning at Eden, I cocked my hip. "My heels are tall, my bikini small. Off to get laid, my friend." She laughed as I sauntered off in Samson's direction.

He spotted me walking toward him. Did a double take. OK, so walking wasn't exactly what I was doing. I mean, who can actually walk in four-inch heels? I took one step at a time *very* carefully. I knew the sway of my hips was exaggerated and just rolled with it. His pace quickened, and I grinned. I stopped by a tree and lazily leaned against it, waiting for him.

"Didn't think you were ever gonna get through with your stodgy old meeting." I pouted.

He didn't respond to my words, but looked my body up and down, scrubbing a hand over his mouth. "I like this outfit."

"Do you?" I stood straighter and did a little pirouette. "I wore it just for you."

"Really."

"Mm-hmm."

"Do that little twirl for me again."

I did, this time slower. I stopped when my back was to him and looked over my shoulder at him. I knew what he'd see, and it nearly made me lose my courage, but I was committed. I'd lost weight. Though he'd made sure I had three good solid meals a day since my captivity, I'd also insisted he help me work out. Fine muscle was starting to show through my legs, abdomen, and back. My arms were more defined. But there were still yellow-green bruises over most of my body in the last stages of healing. I'd been out in the sun as much as I could, hoping a light tan would help hide the bruises until they finished healing, but the few worst ones still persisted in making themselves known. So the view he got of my back was a combination of strength and vulnerability.

I leaned forward, putting my hands against the tree. My ass stuck out, so he had a good view of the thong disappearing into my cheeks. "Lots of possibilities for a position like this," I said as I wiggled my ass a little. "Giving you any ideas?"

"Oh, you could definitely say that," he said, stepping close to me and gripping my hips with his big hands. "I think someone's trying to take advantage of the fact that I've had her in my greedy possession for two weeks and not yet fucked the shit out of her." He brought his hand down hard on one round cheek. "Know that can change. Quickly."

I shivered and shook my ass at him again. "No one said I was gonna stop you if you tried."

"I see." I looked over my shoulder and saw him glancing around, grinding his hips against my ass. His cock pulsed against me, making me ache for him to just unzip his fly, pull my thong aside, and fuck me already. "You're so Goddamn sexy... I love this ass." He knelt behind me and kissed the same cheek he'd slapped. Then he bit down on my flesh sharply enough to make me yelp. "That's it, baby girl. Only reason I'm not fuckin' you right now is because your daddy's somewhere in the fuckin' compound, and even I'm not man enough to risk that."

I giggled. "Scared of my daddy?"

"Honey, I'm sure he's the sweetest man in the world to you. But he's vicious with his enemies. Especially when that enemy threatens his daughter. No. I ain't that brave, sweetheart."

He pulled me up and started to drag me toward the building where our suite was. When he realized there was really no fucking way I could keep up, he just hefted me over his shoulder and took off. I laughed, and he swatted my ass again, lingering on the bare flesh to rub it. Every time he squeezed my ass, he growled.

We passed several club girls on our way to our room, but no one did anything more than wave or laugh at my predicament. I just laughed right along with them. My big, bad biker had reached the point of no return.

Thank fucking God!

* * *

Samson

If that fucker Grady Bassett found out what I was about to do to his daughter, he'd fucking kill me, and I wouldn't blame him. But I was definitely making her mine tonight. She already was, but this would just put the point on it.

When I slammed the door to our room shut and locked it, I felt a tremendous relief. This was finally happening. She wasn't going to run screaming or have a panic attack because I scared her. She wanted this. And I was determined I could give her what she needed without causing her more pain and fear.

I pulled her against me, all that glorious skin filling my palms. Ridding her of that ridiculous bathing suit was as easy as pulling a couple of strings. Getting out of my own clothing proved a little more difficult, but with Charlotte's clever fingers, we managed. What I wasn't expecting was for her to sink to her knees and swallow my cock as eagerly as she did. She couldn't get it all down her throat, but she didn't grip the base and pump what she couldn't get into her mouth. Instead, she gripped my ass and bobbed her head over and over, gagging slightly, but not letting up.

"Fuck, girl! Mother fuck!"

"Mmm…" She took me deeper. Then deeper still. And Goddamn, it felt so fucking good!

"Get off now, Lottie," I said, pushing her away, but she gripped my ass even harder. I had to pull her up by her hair before she finally let go of my cock with a loud "pop."

I shoved her against the wall, pulling one of her knees up. Kneeling, I let it fall over my shoulder while I moved my face between her legs to cover her pussy with my mouth. She sagged against the wall, most of her weight on my shoulder. She gripped my head and hooked her other leg over my shoulder. I stood, sliding her up the wall. When my tongue found her clit, she screamed, riding my mouth by grinding her hips against me. God, she was wet! Her little pussy quivered on my mouth, her cream sweet with her arousal.

"Oh, God! I'm gonna come, Samson!"

"No, you don't," I growled, lifting her down even as she protested, trying to lock her ankles into place. I tossed her onto the bed, then rolled her to her belly. Somehow, I managed to snag a condom from the bedside and roll it on, though it truly pained me to do so. I wanted to go in bare, to fill her with my seed, making her mine. But I couldn't. She might want me, but she wasn't mine.

When she tried to push up, I snagged her hands, pinning them to the small of her back with one of mine. Then I guided my cock inside her until I'd gone as far as I could. She arched her back, meeting my thrust with one of her own.

"Fuck me, Samson," she gasped. "I need you so bad!"

With a swat to her ass, I did as she begged. I let go of her hands to grip her hips, pulling her to me with each surge forward. She was tight, gripping me like a vise. Hot and slick, I moved into her easily, over and over. It was sheer heaven! Nothing had ever been so sweet as the haven of her body. I knew I was going to hell, but having had this slice of heaven, I knew it was worth it.

Sweat slickened her skin, as it did mine. I ran one hand down the curve of her spine lightly just because I could. She arched into me like a little kitten, moaning in pleasure. All the while, I kept moving inside her, needing this pleasure to never end.

When her breathing became erratic, I knew I only had so much time left. When she came, there was no way I'd not come with her. My dick was like a pike, hard as steel. When her muscles gripped and milked me, I had no hope of staving off my orgasm.

"Samson," she gasped.

I snaked my hand around her waist and down to her pussy. Finding her clit, I pressed, rubbing little circles over it, my finger slick with her juices. "That's it, baby," I whispered in her ear. "You need to come, don't you?"

"Yes!" she screamed even as I felt her pussy begin the magical pulsations that signaled her orgasm.

As expected, she gripped my cock in a death grip, her inner muscles rippling and milking me. With a roar or completion, I let go. My cum exploded from me, caught by the thin piece of latex instead of seeking shelter in her body. My vision blurred, and I couldn't seem to breathe for several seconds as my body tensed, all my energy seeming to explode from the head of my dick. When I could finally breathe again, I rolled to my side, taking Charlotte with me. I wrapped my arms around her, my cock still pulsing inside her. "Fuck me," I groaned.

She giggled. "I think I already did that."

"Yeah, baby. You certainly did."

She sighed happily as she let me hold her. God! Was there anything I wouldn't do for this woman? That was an easy question to answer. No. There wasn't. Including killing that fuck, Wrangler. And God knew I wanted that kill. Oh well. I had no control over that. It was El Diablo's decision to make. I'd stand by it either way. So long as the fuck was dead, it made little difference to me.

Chapter Seven

Samson

I didn't get to kill Wrangler. El Diablo let that honor fall to that thorn in my side, Grady Barrett. It was just as well. I was busy with my girl. Charlotte was a warm and giving lover, eager to please and ready to try anything I wanted her to. I was so lost in her magic, I nearly forgot about Barrett. But of course, her father called her every day and, even though he'd agreed to let her stay with me for the time being, I could tell he was pressuring Charlotte to come home.

My phone rang. Speak of the devil…

"Yeah, Barrett. What do you want?"

"My daughter," he growled. "How's she doing?"

"You talk to her every fuckin' day. Don't you know?"

"I do. But I want to hear it from you."

"She still has nightmares occasionally, but her body is healing. She no longer winces when she moves, and there are no bruises on her face. She swims every day and plays with the children. There is rarely a time when there isn't a smile on her face." There. Choke on that. Fucker.

"Good. Sounds like she's ready to come home." The other man made it sound like it was a forgone conclusion she was coming home.

"Not unless she wants to, Barrett. She's happy here. You can come see her whenever you like."

"You ain't fuckin' livin' with my daughter, you fuckin' bastard! And if you've taken advantage of her vulnerability after that bastard kidnapped her, I'll fuckin' kill you myself!"

"Anything she's done, she did on her own. I'm here to make sure no one takes advantage of her. My sister is here to make sure I don't take advantage of her." Lot of good that did. Eden practically pushed us together every chance she got. "Don't like it? Take it up with El Diablo. Still don't like it? Talk to Charlotte. If she wants to leave with you, she's free to go. But if she wants to say, you better bring a fuckin' huge-ass army, because I'm not letting anyone take her away if she doesn't want to leave."

"Look, Samson," Barrett bit out. "I don't think you're a bad man. In fact, I owe you for finding and rescuing her. But she's my daughter."

"I won't go against any man when it comes to his daughter, Barrett. But I also won't let you bully her into leaving if she doesn't want to."

"She's my daughter! I don't have to bully her. If you weren't convincing her she was safer in that fuckin' compound you call a clubhouse, she'd want to come home to be with me. I'm her father! And I'm perfectly capable of keeping her safe."

"She wants to finish her degree, Grady. Some of her classes aren't offered online. I can make sure she has guards looking out for her."

"I can do the same thing," Barrett challenged. "I know my share of ex-military men. Some from your rival club in Palm Springs. I've already been in touch with Thorn at Salvation's Bane. He'll let me hire however many men I need to keep Charlotte safe. Tell me how that's not better than what you're offering her."

I ground my teeth. If I told him she was my woman, Barrett would come after me, and I'd be hard pressed to defend myself. If I didn't, I really had no reason to force the issue. "Talk to her. I already told her if she wanted to leave, I'd take her back to you myself. But I also promised I wouldn't let anyone *make* her leave. Including you."

"If I find you're using her fear to keep her with you, I'll put a bullet in your head, Samson. Overall, I think you're a good man. But I won't hesitate to kill you."

"Look," I said, needing to defuse the situation when I really wanted to tell the bastard to go to hell. "No one said you couldn't come see her. I'm sure she'd love it. You'll see she's happy, healthy, and very well protected. If she wants to go home with you, that's her choice. But she'll have to tell me that's what she wants."

"And I'll be there when she does," Barrett snapped. "You're not in control of her, Samson."

"No," I answered. "She's in control of herself."

I ended the call, wanting to throw the thing through the wall. Fuck! The pisser of it was, Barrett was right. I had no business fucking that girl. Sure, it was her idea. She was the one to push it. But I was older and more experienced. I was in a position of power over her and should have kept my fucking hands off her from the beginning. But, God damn it, she was mine before all this fucking shit! I just hadn't accepted it.

"Everything OK?" Charlotte came up behind me, wrapping her arms around my waist and pressing her cheek to my back.

I turned, pulling her against my chest and hugging her close. "Fine, baby. But I need to go. I have a meeting with El Diablo." I didn't, but I needed to talk with the other man. He wasn't only my president, he was my mentor. My brother. If I was doing Lottie wrong, he wouldn't hesitate to tell me.

"When will you be home?"

"Not sure. May be late. If I can't come home, I'll

call or text."

"OK." She tilted her face up to me for a kiss, and I obliged. God! The taste of her sweet lips always brought me to my knees. This time, it was worse. I wasn't sure there was any way I could let her go. No matter if it was the right thing to do.

As I left, I gave her what I hoped was a reassuring wink, but I could tell she knew something was wrong. Outside the door, Iron and Tank were waiting. "Stay here. Not sure when I'll be back."

"We'll watch over her, brother."

"If Eden comes to stay with her, make sure you get two other brothers with you. I don't want any accidents."

"What are you expecting to happen to these girls, Samson?" Iron wasn't condescending, just genuinely curious. He seemed like an easygoing, pussy-chasing pretty boy, but he was all business when it came to protecting the club and anyone in it.

"Nothing. I'm just making sure and keeping my promises."

"Wrangler's not a threat. You think someone else might be?"

"Yeah," I said with a sigh. "Her fuckin' father."

Instantly Iron stood straighter. "Don't worry, brother. El Diablo's given him a wide latitude, but I can keep him corralled if you want me to."

"No. I don't want to keep them apart. I just don't want him trying to slip her out. She goes nowhere unless she talks to me first. Not even outside the compound. You get me?"

"Understood."

Instructions delivered, I stomped my way to El Diablo's office. This time of day he was always there. I found him frowning down at his phone before shrugging his shoulders and laying it back on the desk. He looked up and grinned brightly when I walked in.

"Ah! Good. I wondered if you'd be in here." He nodded to his phone. "Seems the good sheriff is a shade upset."

"You gonna let him take Charlotte?"

El Diablo shrugged. "She's his daughter. Tell me why I shouldn't."

"I promised her I wouldn't let anyone make her go anywhere she didn't want to go. Including her father. She expressly said he'd try to make her go back home. Right now, she doesn't want to."

"What about you, Samson? What do you want?" El Diablo didn't look shrewd or devious or anything. He looked genuinely curious. So I just laid it out for him.

"She's my world. Not sure I could let her go even if she wanted me to. I mean, I wouldn't keep her prisoner, but I'm not sure I'd be able to keep myself from following her."

"I see." He sighed. "Well, Grady Bassett isn't a man to just abandon his daughter. No matter what her wishes are, you may have a fight on your hands."

"Well aware of that," I bit out, growling as I ran my hands over my head in frustration. "I can't fight her dad. Not and keep her."

El Diablo chuckled and spread his hands. "Then don't."

"Don't? What does that mean?"

"Don't fight him. Just be the man Charlotte needs you to be."

I sighed, sinking into a nearby chair. Needing to change the subject, I asked, "Wrangler been disposed of?"

"I believe the good sheriff is taking care of that

now. I find it hard to believe the man has such a vicious streak in him when he's known in Glades County as such a good man. I suppose we all have a side the world doesn't see."

"Or ignores."

"Exactly."

"I need to check in with Chief and Loki. They were double-checking the cleanup."

"Hum… Well, I suppose if you think that's the best use of your time."

That caught me off guard. "You don't want me to follow up on this? If any part of that scene is discovered, we're all fucked."

"You know Rycks is on it. You can put as many men as you think necessary on it. With the situation you're in with your girl, I'd have thought you'd want to stay."

"I do, God damn it! But I can't!"

He raised an eyebrow at me. "I fail to see why not. She's your woman."

"Because she needs sweet and gentle. Do I fucking look like sweet and gentle?"

"No. You look like a man who becomes whatever his woman needs. Were you too rough with her?"

"She says no, but how could I not be? And I shouldn't be fuckin' her anyway. Not yet."

"So why did you?"

"Because she tricked me! She seduced me. She said she loved it, but how can I be sure she's not just saying that to keep me as her protector? I don't care if she uses me like that if she needs to, but I don't want to hurt her in the process. She's likely too afraid I'll leave her if she tells me I'm scaring her."

"Oh, she seems like a shrinking violet to me, too," El Diablo said sarcastically. "To hear Loki tell it, she fought you like a wildcat in that basement before she realized it was you."

I sighed, feeling more weary than I ever had. "She deserves better than me. She deserves someone her father approves of so there's no friction in her life. Of all the people in her life, she needs her father the most right now."

"Maybe she needs you just as much."

I wasn't so sure. Instead of voicing my doubts, I nodded. "I'll check in on Charlotte, then I need to touch base with Loki and Chief." Before he could protest, I held up my hand. "I know Rycks is perfectly capable, but as vice president of the club, it's my duty to see this done properly. I'll tell Charlotte where I'm going and that I'll be gone a while. I'll also keep in touch with her. Shotgun got some kind of scrambling software from Giovanni at Argent Tech. I'll make sure our phones are fitted with it and that it works before heading out. There will be no way to track me if I call or text."

"Do what you feel is right, then," El Diablo stood and extended a hand to me. Seemed rather formal, but then again, El Diablo could be that way. I stood and took his hand. "Make sure you explain things to her, Samson. We've all fucked up with our women this way. Don't you do it, too."

"Understood, boss."

I made my way back to our suite where I found Lottie curled up on the window seat. She'd made a nest of blankets and looked out over the back of the property to the sea beyond. When she looked back at me, I lost my breath. The woman was so stunningly beautiful I couldn't imagine any man letting her go willingly.

"Hey," she said, giving me a small smile.

"Everything good with your meeting?"

"Yeah, baby," I said, crossing to her and sitting on the edge next to her. I reached out and tucked a curl behind her ear. Instead of flinching as she had a few weeks ago, she leaned into my touch, capturing my hand with hers and turning her face into my palm.

"But you have to go somewhere. Don't you?"

I sighed. "Yeah. I do. I won't lie and say I can't get anyone else to do it. I can. In fact, there are several people already on the task. But it's my responsibility. Much as I want to stay with you, I need to take care of this myself. Do you understand?"

She nodded. "I get the feeling you've been putting off a lot of things because of me. I don't want you to do that."

"I'll be back as quickly as I can." I handed her a phone equipped with the scrambling software Shotgun had given me. "I'll contact you with this phone. If you need me, only use this one. It prevents anyone from being able to trace the calls." This next part nearly ripped out my guts. But I had to say it. She had to know it was best if she at least considered going home with her father. "I want you to promise me something," I said, taking her hands in mine.

"Anything. What is it?"

"When this is over, your father wants you to go home with him. I'll always be here for you, and I'll never leave you unguarded. But I think it might be best if you went home. I'm asking for you to give it some serious thought."

She sucked in a breath, her face going pale. "What?"

I sighed, my gut clenching in protest, but plowed on. "There will never be another woman for me, Charlotte. You're it for me. But I'm, what? Seventeen or so years your senior? I don't want you to feel crowded or like I'm taking away your choices. I've kept you behind closed doors since I brought you here, and I'd continue to do so. It doesn't feel like it because this place is so huge, but how long has it been since you went outside those gates?"

"I don't need to go outside," she said, tears gathering in her eyes. "Not because I'm afraid, but because I don't have a reason. I have everything I need right here."

"Just think about it. Your dad has plans in place for guards for you until you adjust and feel safe. You can go home."

"You said you wouldn't let anyone make me leave." Tears glistened in her eyes, and I could see the effort it took for her to hold them back.

"And no one will. I'm just asking you to really think about it." I kissed her fingers. God, if my brothers could see me now, they'd call me a pussy. But I was putty for this girl when no woman had ever been able to capture my heart. "I wouldn't suggest it if I didn't truly believe it was what was best for you."

She stared at me for long moments, searching for something I knew I couldn't give her. "OK," she whispered. "I'll think about it."

"Your dad loves you, Lottie," I said. "He doesn't want you latching on to anyone simply because we were there to rescue you. You'd be miserable in the long run, and I absolutely will not have that."

Charlotte moved to sit up on her knees and threw her arms around me. I wasn't expecting it, but I welcomed it. I felt her slight body trembling and knew she was crying, which broke my heart. I didn't want her to hurt. But I'd rather she hurt a little now than a lot later. At the same time, I knew I'd never be whole without her.

Fuck.

We clung to each other for a long time. I let her set the pace. I wanted to make love to her before I left, but didn't dare. I'd already done too much in that regard. She thought she wanted me. I knew she was growing to love me, which I was so grateful for. At the same time, that love could turn to heartache in a short time. She needed a younger man. One who could relate to her better.

When she finally pulled away, she wiped her eyes with the back of her hand. "Promise me you'll be careful?"

"I swear it, honey."

"I'm not leaving until I see you again. No matter what. Even Dad can't make me."

"No one said you had to. I just want you to think about it. And I *will* see you when I get back. No matter what."

Leaving her in that moment was the hardest thing I'd ever done. Not only was she upset, but I could feel her slipping through my fingers. Not because she wanted to be gone, but because I knew it was the right thing for her.

Heading to the cleanup site, I climbed on my Harley and left the compound. My brothers had their orders on caring for her so she was safe. My only problem was how to deal with this without breaking her heart.

Or my own.

* * *

Charlotte

Samson was breaking my heart. It had been two weeks since he'd told me I should consider going back with my dad. I'd steadfastly refused, and he'd kept his promise to not let anyone take me away if I didn't want to go. He'd also not encouraged any kind of relationship with me. Sure, we'd had sex before, but now, he shut it down before it went beyond a few kisses even though I'd practically begged him to take me again. Every time he denied me, he looked like it gutted him, but he didn't reverse himself.

Someone else keeping a promise to me was Eden. Any time Samson wasn't with me, she was at my side. Like the sister I never had. To be honest, I'm not sure what I'd have done if she hadn't been there. She always seemed to know how to make things, if not better, at least tolerable.

Like now. We were drinking Margaritas by the pool (heavy on the tequila) and bitching to each other how intolerable men were. While it didn't help my heartache, it certainly helped to vent a little. Besides, having Samson's sister agree with me he was being difficult made me feel vindicated.

"I can't believe he's ignoring me like this," I groused. I was more than a little drunk and knew I was being whiny, but I felt whiny. I felt rejected. Perhaps, given our age and experience differences, I should have expected he'd lose interest, but he'd been so sweet otherwise. "I mean, he's always nice. He is always there for dinner. He calls and texts when he's not with me. I've not gone to sleep without him being next to me. *In a fucking chair*! If nightmares wake me, he's there. If I have to get up in the night for any reason, he's there. Unfailingly protective and gentle, but always at a distance. What the fuck am I doing wrong?" I hiccupped, more than a little drunk as I poured out my heart to Eden.

"Girl, I don't know. That man is gone on you. I

have no idea why he's doing this. It's almost as if he wants you to go, but I know for a fact he doesn't." Eden wasn't as drunk as me, but she was still more than a couple sheets to the wind. "Do you know where he is now?"

I shrugged. "He said something about having to take care of business at Salvation's Bane. So I guess he's in Palm Springs." We sat in silence for a bit. I was about to doze off in the warm sun when a thought struck me. "You don't think he's there with club girls. Do you?"

"Samson? Nah. He's not into club girls. Besides, he's with you."

"No. I don't think he is," I said. My belly tensed up even more. "Maybe he went there so he could scratch an itch without me finding out. He may not want me sexually, but he'd never hurt me intentionally. As long as I'm here, he won't let me see him with a woman, or put one in my path where she could say something."

Eden just looked at me, her face hard. That look was all I needed to know about what she thought. That was exactly what her brother would do. Taking out my phone, I sent off a text to Samson.

Me: *Sry for throwin myself @ u. Goin home with Dad tmorow.*

It was a couple of minutes before he responded.

Samson: *We'll talk when I get home.*

Me: *Nothin to tlk bout.*

Samson: *What are you doing?*

I thought about not answering that one but shrugged. What the fuck? Why not?

Me: *Gettin drnk w/Eden.*

When there was no response, I set my phone down and sighed. He was probably happily making plans on how to celebrate the ol' ball and chain rolling back down the hill away from him. Then Eden's phone rang. She looked at the screen and scowled.

"Motherfucker," she muttered before answering. "Don't want to talk to you right now, Samson." That perked me up. I sat up straighter in the lounge chair. "It's none of your business what we're doing. We're both able to make our own decisions." She gave me a firm nod, grinning as she did. "Hey. Don't look at me. I'm not the one telling her to leave. She's the sister I never had. My best friend. And you're pushing her away!"

Just hearing Eden lay it out there sliced a deep gash in my heart. He was pushing me away. Why? Maybe he really was tired of me.

"Honey, if he's tired of you, then he's the most stupid man I've ever met," Eden said as she continued her conversation with Samson. Had I said that out loud? I poured myself another Margarita. Eden continued her conversation with Samson while I closed my eyes as I sipped my drink. The sun would normally have been a balm to my worries. The alcohol made my head buzz pleasantly, and the sounds of the sea beyond the walls of the compound would normally have soothed me. Now, it just made me that much more miserable.

How many times had I sat here by the pool with Samson talking and laughing? I loved seeing the fine lines around his eyes as they crinkled with his smile.

"I told you, it's none of your business where we are," Eden snapped. "It's your fault she's leaving in the first Goddamned place! Why would I want you here with us?" There was a pause while Samson spoke, then Eden continued. "I'm making it my mission on this earth to find someone who will give Lottie what she needs. I mean, you were her first choice, but you're a pussy who's afraid of her dad. So yeah. I'm finding someone more worthy of her courage."

I sat up, dropping my glass. It shattered on the concrete. "I'm going to pack my things, then I'm calling Dad." I sighed. "I can't do this."

Eden turned to me, snagging my hands. "Yes, you can! You take this fight to him. Take it to him and don't give in until you get what you want! Look," she said. "Repeat after me. I don't need a pussy."

"I don't need a pussy," I dutifully repeated.

"I need my pussy eaten."

I blinked several times, but when she squeezed my hands, I parroted her. "I need my..." The beginnings of a giggle started, and I faltered. "My pussy..." I couldn't stop it. I grinned and laughed. "Eaten!"

We both dissolved into giggles.

"What the hell is going on here?" a voice boomed from across the yard.

"Motherfucker," Eden muttered. "I played right into his hands."

"What does that mean?"

"It means, he probably had Shotgun locating us. Through my conversation with him."

Samson approached us, stopping to glance down at the broken glass, then my bare feet. Without a word, he lifted me into his arms. He looked back at Eden. "You and I will have a talk later."

Eden just grinned and waved at me. I was lucky to have her on my side. Looked like Samson was the one who played into her hands. Not the other way around.

Chapter Eight

Samson

It didn't take long to get... home. Home was where I'd spent most of the last six weeks or so with Charlotte. She wasn't going to her daddy's -- she wasn't leaving me. I thought I could handle it, but I knew there was just no way. There was no way in this world I would ever be home if Charlotte wasn't with me.

"What the hell do you think you're doing?" she bit out, kicking and squirming until I let her down.

I made sure I was between her and the door so I could shut and lock it before she made a break for it. "We need to talk."

"We did! It went something like, 'You need to go home to your daddy.'"

Yeah. I'd fucked up. "You do," I said. "But I'm not sure I can let you."

"Oh!" She fumed, looking around until she found something sufficiently hard. The TV remote. Then she flung it at my head.

I gave her a dark look as I stalked toward her, but even though a flicker of unease flitted over her face, Charlotte lifted her chin and stared me down. Yeah. I was putty in her hands.

With a heavy groan, I simply pulled her into my arms and held her tightly. She actually let me. For a full minute. Then her breathing became erratic and a sob broke free. Charlotte shoved me away as hard as she could. I let her because I was afraid she was having a panic attack. "You bastard!" she screamed at me. "You fucking bastard!"

"Yeah. I got that," I said, knowing this wasn't going to be easy. Or smooth.

"You don't touch me for all this time, letting me know I need to get away from you, now this? You're a fucking asshole, Samson! A motherfuckin' asshole!"

"I know, baby. I'm sorry. I can't keep you, but I can't let you go."

"Then tell me why!" she demanded. "Either come clean, or I'm walking while I still have some semblance of pride left!"

"Look," he said, scrubbing a hand over his face. "Your dad hates me."

"He doesn't hate you," she muttered. "He hates every guy I date."

"Yeah? Well, you and I ain't datin'. You think he'd approve of everything we've already done? He threatened to kill me if I took advantage of you after your attack. And by 'taking advantage of' he meant fuckin'. Which I did."

"You did, because I wanted it!" she screamed, her fists balled at her side. "He doesn't get to tell me what I want or need. I wouldn't have gone to any other man, Samson. Just you. Only you."

"I understand that, baby. But, believe me when I tell you, he will *never* understand."

"How do you know? My daddy loves me! He's only ever wanted me to be happy."

"I know because, when our parents died and I was in charge of Eden, she was young enough she was almost like my daughter. I was barely eighteen, but she was just a toddler." I scrubbed a hand over my face several times. "I know what it's like to watch some man whose intentions toward Eden are less than honorable. I also know she's her own woman, and I can't run off every man who looks her way. Doesn't make it any easier to keep from killing the motherfucker."

I reached out for Charlotte and, thankfully, she took my hand, letting me pull her against me. "I can't defy a man who loves his daughter. And he might respect me in some things, but he's a man. He knows my interest in you isn't just to keep you safe." He sighed. "Hell, I still have trouble with Eden and her choices. She works cam shows with my brothers. She and Iron currently have a semi-regular thing going, and it's all I can do not to gut the motherfucker sometimes. But I know Iron. I know every brother in this place. They like to have fun, but they're good men. They'd never intentionally hurt Eden. Other than Iron, she never hooked up outside the cam team and only during scenes. That's her choice. Doesn't mean I like it."

"Doesn't mean you hurt the men, either," she muttered. "Dad will respect my choice."

"Look at your situation with me, honey. I've got to be close to twenty years your senior. Iron is older than Eden, but not by that much. If someone that much older than her was pokin' his head around, I'd probably shoot the bastard and ask questions later. I don't want to put your daddy in that situation. Because, honey, I'd never let him take you from me."

"So? Don't! Don't let him take me! I don't want to go back. Not because I wouldn't feel safe or because I don't love my dad. Because *you're my choice*!"

"That can't happen, Lottie," he said softly.

"Are you really afraid of him, then?"

She looked so bewildered and hurt, I wanted to pull her into my arms. But there was no way for that to happen now. Not if I was going to do the right thing and give her up. God! I wanted her so fucking bad! "No, baby. I'm not. But I can't kill him when he comes for you. I'll stand by my promise. I won't let him take you away if you don't want to go. But, no matter what I want, we can't be together."

"Do I not have any say in the matter?"

"About that? No."

There was a half-empty beer bottle sitting on the coffee table she picked up and hurled at me. "Bastard!" Then she threw a heavy ashtray. Then a lamp from one end table. "You motherfucking bastard!"

"Baby." I wanted to soothe her but had no idea how to go about it. I couldn't keep her, no matter how much I wanted to.

"Don't you baby me! You think my dad'll be mad if we get together? How do you think he'll react when he finds out you broke my heart?"

I tilted my head at her. I couldn't have heard that right. "What's your heart got to do with it, Lottie?"

"I love you, you fuckin' asshole!" She threw the other lamp at me. That one was bigger and harder for her to throw, but also harder for me to bat away. "I've loved you since the first night we fucked!"

I shook my head. "That was infatuation. You'd never had a real lover before, and I made you feel good."

"God! You're so stupid! You think I don't know what love is? I watched my father devote his entire existence to my mother before she died! I saw the way he looked at her, the way he protected her and cherished her. He took any little thing he thought she might want and made it a reality. Why? Just to see her smile. I knew I wanted a man to do that for me. Since you brought me here, you've been doing it. Hell, even that one night, you gave me anything I wanted and pushed me to ask you for more. You think I don't know you love me? It's written all over your face! In everything you do for me!"

I started to say something, but she held up her hand.

"You know what? Fuck you. Fuck you and your stupid scruples. I'm fucking outta here!"

She tried to stomp past me to the door, but I simply wrapped my arms around her waist and scooped her up. I took her to the bedroom with her screeching and thrashing all the way. When I set her down, she started hitting me. Which only made me want her more. "You love me," I said. It was such an inane statement. After everything she'd just told me, I felt like I sounded as stupid as she'd named me.

"That's what I fucking said!" she screamed at me, looking around the room. Probably for something else to throw at me.

"Get your fuckin' clothes off," I said, stripping off my shirt. I toed off my boots and shoved my jeans and boxers to the floor. She just gaped at me.

"If you think I'm fucking you, you can just think -- oh!"

I grabbed her to me and fastened my lips to hers.

She fought me, but only for dominance. Her fingers dug into my shoulder and neck, holding me to her. Her tongue met mine thrust for thrust, which just made me harder. I grabbed her shirt and whipped it over her head. She shoved off her shorts and panties, her breathing as erratic as mine.

"You're such an asshole!" she yelled before lunging toward me. Before I realized what she was doing, she slapped me. Hard.

"Oh, it's on, baby," I said, snagging her around the waist and tossing her to the bed.

"Bastard!" She shoved me hard as I lowered myself on top of her. It caught me off guard, and she managed to shove me to the side. I rolled to my back and she was on top of me, straddling my hips. "You're such a dork," she said as she guided my cock inside her. "Such a fucking bastard!"

"And you're beautiful," I growled, gripping her hips lightly as she settled herself. The look of ecstasy on her face was an awesome sight. When she moved on me, her hips did a slow undulation before picking up a faster, harder rhythm. She looked down into my face, her fierce pride and love obvious. She also looked almost lost. Her eyes were bright with tears. One tracked down her cheek like an accusation.

So I swatted her ass.

"What the fuck, Samson?"

"That's for not telling me you loved me sooner."

"I take it back! I hate you!"

"No take backs, little darlin'." I grinned up at her before rolling to settle her beneath me. "You want this?" I asked. "You want me fuckin' you?" When she nodded, I shook my head. "I need words, Lottie."

"Yes," she gasped. "I want you to fuck me."

"Good." And I gave her what she asked for.

Over and over I surged into her, wrapping my arms around her. Her legs gripped my hips to lock at her ankles at the small of my back. She held on with all her strength, gasping with every move I made.

"Samson!" Charlotte screamed my name, her nails raking over my back like little claws.

"You're gonna come, Lottie. You're gonna come on my cock and milk me dry, you hear me?"

"Yes! Oh, God! Samson!" With a long, shrill scream, Charlotte did exactly what I told her to. She came and came until she took me with her. When I did, it was deep inside her. Right where I'd wanted to be since the first fucking night I'd had her. She was beautiful. Passionate. Smart. Beautiful... *Mine.*

Chapter Nine

Samson

I was gonna get my ass handed to me, and I deserved everything I got. Didn't mean I was backing down or giving up Charlotte. She was mine. Her daddy could just learn to live with it. Or try to kill me. I was betting on the latter. He wouldn't succeed, but I had no doubt he'd try.

I kissed Charlotte's temple, leaving her asleep in our bed. I didn't want to leave her, but I had to do this now. If I was a good man, I'd take her home and never look back. Fuck. If I was a good man I wouldn't be here with her in my bed right now.

Pale sunlight filtered through the blinds as I dressed. The light shone on all that lovely hair of Charlotte's, highlighting gold strands through the chestnut. My chest ached with how beautiful she was. My woman. Yes. It was like a weight had been lifted from my shoulders. This was what I was supposed to do. What I was supposed to be. I was Charlotte's man. And she was my woman.

Determined to see this settled today, I dressed and picked up my phone. I texted Eden, asking her to come stay with Charlotte while I was gone. Not surprisingly, she was close. Since she'd promised Charlotte she'd stay with her when I couldn't, my sister had been true to her word. It wasn't a full minute before Eden rounded the corner. Her eyes were a bit bloodshot, and she smelled like a winery, but she had a smile on her face.

"She finally makin' an honest man outta you, Samson?"

"You're a smartass sometimes, you know that, kid?"

"Ain't been a kid in a long time." She grinned. "I'm a shade hung over, but I'll get Lyric to come sit with us. If I get sick, she'll be here to take care of us both."

I grinned, then pulled my sister in for a hug. "I'm lucky to have you, Eden. Don't ever change."

"I'll always be here for you, bro. You and my new sister. Thank you for bringing her to me."

I snorted. "Yeah? Well, she's mine. Don't forget that."

"She's mine, too. As your little sister, I demand you share."

"Go. Watch over my woman while I confront her father."

"Good luck."

"Yeah," I said, releasing her. "I have a feeling I might need it on this one."

My next call was to El Diablo. He needed to know my plans since it could impact the club. "Why not just invite him here?" he asked. "Less likely he'd try to kill you if you're surrounded by your club."

"Because I'd be surrounded by my club?" I chuckled. "Much as I'd like to, I can't."

"No. I don't suppose you can. I don't approve, but I understand. I do think you should take someone with you. Shadow, perhaps? He's not exactly Black Reign, but he's a big motherfucker. Might deter violence."

"No. I'll take my beating like a man. Barrett will be out for blood, but I want to meet him in neutral territory. I figured Tito's would be as good a place as any."

"Just make sure no one gets caught in the crossfire."

I snorted. "Right. You honestly think Marge or

Elena would let that happen?"

"Agreed, but don't you put them in that position. If they withhold the Marge special from me, I'm holding you personally responsible."

Yeah. It was a real fear.

"Understood."

The call to Sheriff Bassett went smoother than I thought. He agreed to meet me, no questions asked. Which didn't really bode well for me. Bassett wasn't a dumbass. He knew what was going on, and he wasn't showing his hand.

Bassett actually got to the diner before me, taking a seat in the corner so I had to put my back to the door. Something the other man knew I'd hate. Still, I did it. Call it a show of trust or respect. Marge brought us both coffee and left us alone, seeming to sense we weren't there for breakfast.

We sat there a good hour, neither saying a word. There was still the breakfast rush, and the last thing we wanted to do was to cause a scene. At least, not yet.

"I'm surprised Tito lets you and your MC in the place," Bassett commented over the rim of his coffee cup. "Seems he and Marge know what's about to happen. I'd think they'd prefer it if you all just... went away." The sheriff sounded as menacing as he looked.

"Make no mistake --" Marge said as she approached to refill our cups, "-- these boys know where the line is and not to cross it. We'd never ban them entirely, but I'd take away the Marge Specials, and no one would be happy about that." She nodded at Bassett. "That goes for you too, Grady. We like you, but there's a line." She didn't smile.

"Not sure which one of you three we should fear the most, Marge," I said, grinning at the older lady. "But I damn sure don't want to have my specials taken away."

Marge looked from one of us to the other. Then focused on me. "How's little Charlotte doing? She's too sweet a girl to have gone through what she has. You still looking after her?"

I winced. Marge knew exactly why we were here. Likely El Diablo had given her a heads-up. Or maybe my sister. "She's much better. And yes. I'm still looking after her."

She nodded firmly. "Good." Then she patted my shoulder lightly. "You're good for each other. She looks at you the same way you look at her." She smiled. "With so much love it warms the room." When she walked away, Bassett looked like he might kill me.

"You son of a bitch."

"She's my world. I love her more than my next breath. She loves me too. Don't believe me? Come to the Black Reign compound and talk to her. She'll tell you the same thing."

Bassett glanced around us. Even though I couldn't see most of the room, I knew most everyone was gone. The lull before the lunch rush was beginning at last. When his gaze fell back on me, I sighed. The next few minutes were gonna be rough.

"What have you done to my daughter, you fuckin' bastard?" He bit out the words between clenched teeth. His fists clenched tightly on the table.

"I haven't done anything to her other than love her. She's mine."

"Tough shit," Bassett said, getting up. "She was mine first."

The first punch landed with blinding force. The second and I tasted blood.

"Oh, no you don't!" Elena said, emerging from the back shaking a wooden spoon. "You start roughhousing, you take it outside!"

"You heard the lady, boys," Tito said. "Out with you!"

Bassett grabbed me by the shirt and tried to haul me outside, but I shrugged him off and gave him a shove out the door. The battle that ensued next was one for the ages. Sheriff Grady Bassett and I pummeled each other in the parking lot for close to half an hour.

"How long do you think they'll keep this up?" The familiar female voice caught my attention. Which only let Bassett land another punch to my ribs.

"They're both strong men in their prime," another woman said. "I'd say they could go for hours if they conserve their strength." I was certain that was Marge talking. The other was my sister.

"Eden!" I tried to focus on Bassett, but if Eden was here, then Charlotte was along. "What are you doing here?" Bassett landed another punch, this time to my jaw.

"Watching two dumbasses pummel each other," she called back after a swig from her Coke. "Lyric is with Charlotte. She's waiting for you to come back home." Eden raised her phone in salute to me. "But don't worry. I'm getting all this on video so we can pop some popcorn and watch it later. She won't miss a thing." She and Marge had pulled up chairs and were both watching us.

I glanced at Bassett who was scowling at my sister. "What's she playing at?"

"Who, me?" Eden looked as innocent as a babe, even batting her eyelashes at him. "I'm just showing my new sister how bravely her man is fighting for her against the mean ol' tyrant."

"Tyrant?" The other man looked affronted. "I'm protecting my daughter from a lecherous old bastard!"

"Mmm," Marge grunted, looking both of us up and down. "I do so love a man covered in sweat..." She winked at me.

"Agreed," Eden said, eyeing Bassett like she'd like to lick all that sweat from his body. I immediately stepped in front of him, giving Eden a warning look. "Good," she said brightly. "I have your attention." I glanced back at Bassett, who moved up to stand beside me. Then Eden continued. "Lottie is staying with Samson at Black Reign," she said, looking directly at Bassett. "It's what she wants. Since she is the only woman I'd ever approve to be with my big brother, I'll do anything I have to, to keep her happy." She glanced at me briefly before continuing. "Including nailing his balls to the wall if he hurts her. But I'm pretty sure you know Samson would never hurt her. In any way. You want my opinion?"

Bassett snorted. "Why not? What's your opinion, smart ass?"

Eden didn't hesitate. She just pointed a finger at Bassett and plowed on. "You, sir. Need to get laid. Badly." Again, she eyed him up and down. "Come see me when you're ready." Then she tipped the Coke can and swigged the rest down before sauntering over to her car and peeling out of the parking lot.

"Well, then," Marge said as she stood gracefully. "If you boys will take the chairs back in, I think we're done here." Bassett and I looked at each other. He gave me a hard, angry look, but neither of us said anything. Marge must have taken that as her cue to finish scolding us. "Now, once you put those chairs where they belong, you both have your orders. Samson, go let Lottie know you've cleared everything with her father and she doesn't have to worry about leaving the place she considers her home. It will put her mind at ease, the poor dear. And you, Sheriff Bassett?" She leaned close to him, poking him in the chest with her finger. "Go get laid."

I bared my teeth at the bastard, but he only raised an eyebrow. Yeah. The irony wasn't lost on either of us.

* * *

Charlotte

The second Samson walked through the door to our home at the clubhouse, I jumped up and threw myself into his arms. I had no idea what had happened, but I was not letting my dad get into his head. If anyone was gonna mess with him, it was gonna be me. It took a few moments to realize he'd been in a fight. Another couple moments to put two and two together to get that it had been my dad he'd fought. Or rather, judging by the beating his face had taken, it had been my dad he'd let pummel him.

"You coulda fought back," I muttered, giving him a lingering if gentle kiss on his swollen lip.

"I did. Fucker's just that good," he grumbled, holding me to him.

"I'm not leaving, Samson," I said fiercely, pulling back and making him look me in the eyes. I wanted him to understand. This was it for me. I was staying with him.

"No. You fuckin' ain't! You even think it, and I'll turn you over my knee and paddle your ass till you can't sit for a month. I didn't take this beatin' just for you to run off."

I couldn't help it. I squealed. Might have been in his ear, but he didn't say a word. Just held me as tight as I held him.

He filled me in on the events at Tito's and the

byplay. How his sister and Marge had come to the rescue and defused the situation before it got too out of hand.

"Unfortunately, my sister is taunting your dad. I'm not sure how I feel about this."

I laughed until my belly hurt and my cheeks ached. "I imagine this is going to get more uncomfortable for you before it gets better."

"Quite possibly," he acknowledged. He did not look amused.

Then there was a knock at the door. We both groaned.

"What the everlasting fuck?" Samson muttered as he opened the door. Eden stood there, grinning from ear to ear. "Can't I have a moment's peace, Eden?" He sounded long suffering, but I could hear the affection for his sister in Samson's voice.

"Sure," she said. "Just not right now." Eden hiked a thumb over her shoulder. "There's a certain sexy sheriff in the common room wanting a word with you both."

"Dad's here?"

"Yep," Eden said, grinning. "He keeps giving me weird looks. I think I may have broke him."

"Oh, I gotta see this," I said, scrambling to get my shoes on.

"Do we have to?" Samson sighed. "I kinda had plans."

"The only plan you get to make is a hot bath and bed," I said, looking at his beaten face. "I'm sure the rest of you doesn't look or feel much better."

"Not what I had planned, but I'll agree if you'll get in the bath with me."

"You comin' or not?" Eden asked.

"Give us a fuckin' second," Samson growled.

"Can't a man get some sympathy in peace?"

"Later," I said, going up on my tiptoes to kiss his mouth. "I'll give you all the sympathy you can stand."

"Holdin' you to that."

As we entered the common room, I saw my father talking with El Diablo. The other man looked nearly as bad as Samson, so I forgave them both. I ran to my dad and threw myself into his arms. Dad hugged me fiercely, and I knew he'd only had my best interests at heart. Just like always.

"I love you, pumpkin," he said softly. "You sure this is what you want? He's a rough guy."

"Rough, but good, Dad. Yes. He's what I want. If he ever gets to not be what I want, you can reevaluate and kick his ass then."

He chuckled warmly before putting me down. When he glanced over my shoulder to Samson, he scowled. "Just so we're clear, Samson," he said. "You break her heart or hurt her in any way, I'll fuckin' kill you."

"I can respect that," Samson answered with a nod. "Same goes for my sister."

Dad scowled. "Woman's a menace. In any case, you don't have anything to worry about there. She's too young for me. I have no intention of being around her unless she's with Charlotte."

"Oh yeah?" Eden said, blowing a bubble with her gum. "We'll see about that." She gave him a wink. Then uncrossed and recrossed her legs where she sat on the barstool facing my father. He frowned at her. She just grinned.

"Fuckin' menace," Dad muttered.

That evening, there was a party. No particular reason. Just… party! Unfortunately for Samson, there was a contingent of Salvation's Bane members there.

Apparently, it's considered bad form in the MC world for the vice president not to show up for these things when there's another club present. I didn't care, though. The party was a fucking blast! Not only was there plenty of food, but it looked like one huge sex fest. While I had all the sex I wanted or needed from Samson, I was getting lots of ideas for later.

"Good to see you, Samson." The man was just like all the rest. Tall, tattooed, bearded, and scary-looking. He had a pleasant smile.

Samson took his hand in a firm shake. "Thorn, this is my woman, Charlotte."

Thorn glanced at me and nodded. "My woman's at the bar with the other ol' ladies." He turned and motioned to a woman who immediately got up and walked in our direction. She smiled warmly, making me feel at ease. "Mariana, this is Charlotte. She's the woman who's tamed Samson here." Thorn clapped Samson on the shoulder and everyone else laughed. "Why don't you introduce her to the others?"

I met several women from Salvation's Bane, all of them friendly and completely devoted to their men. From what I could tell, the men were completely devoted to them, too. The men they pointed out as theirs might have backed off to give the women space, but they had eyes on them, ready to come to their side if needed. It warmed my heart. Because Samson looked at me the same way.

Eden was on the other side of the bar taking selfies. With a series of different men from Black Reign. And she was doing it topless.

"Eden," I called across the bar, waving her over. When she just grinned at me and continued, I shrugged. I didn't care if anyone overheard. "What the hell are you doing?"

"Stirring the hornet's nest," she replied with a grin. Then continued snapping pics. Was she sending them to someone?

Lyric giggled. "That one is trouble."

"With a capital T," added Mariana. "I bet life around here isn't boring."

"Not at all," I said with a laugh.

The door to the common room burst open. It turned heads, but everyone just threw up a hand in greeting. Someone tossed a beer at the newcomer, and he caught it with a deft hand. Was that... my father? He looked wild. On the verge of being out of control. His hair was nearly standing on end, as if he'd been scrubbing his hands through it constantly. His eyes were wide and intent, a predator looking for his prey.

It was obvious the moment he spotted who he was looking for. His head snapped around and his gaze locked onto one spot, ignoring everyone else around him. Stalking toward the person he'd focused on, he seemed to have a singular purpose. To reach the object he was about to claim as his.

Eden.

"Oh, shit," I muttered. "You've had it now, Eden."

The other woman looked at me and winked before turning to face the menace coming toward her. The two men she'd been taking selfies with had abandoned her, though I saw Iron from across the room take several steps forward before backing off.

A large, heavy hand landed on my shoulder, pulling me close. I'd recognize that intoxicating scent anywhere. Samson wrapped me in his arms and kissed my lips gently. When he pulled back, he gave me a grin. "You better not let your father hurt my sister."

"He wouldn't," I assured him. The grin on

Samson's face told me he believed me, but also that he wasn't so sure, given the circumstances.

Eden saw him coming and tucked her phone into her back pocket, picking up her drink and taking a hefty pull. She'd barely set the bottle down when my dad reached her. He didn't say anything, just scooped her up over his shoulder and swatted her ass when she protested too loudly.

"You fucking bastard!" she shouted. "Put me down!"

Dad responded by swatting her ass again. I was on the other side of the bar. While not that far away, it seemed as if Dad wasn't interested in too much small talk. He gave Samson a hard look. I looked up at Samson to find him shaking his head but gave a sigh of resignation before finally returning Dad's steely gaze with one of his own. Then Dad shifted his gaze to me. He raised a hand to point to the cell I had set on the bar. I grinned, knowing what he was doing.

I picked up my phone and shot off a quick text to Eden as Dad turned and carried her out. She protested all the way. When her phone went off, Dad snagged it from her back pocket and handed it to her. Eden promptly hit in him in the head with it twice before Dad simply swatted her ass again. He seemed to love doing that, and more than once his touch lingered on Eden's bottom, and he rubbed it almost lovingly. I should probably be torn up about this, but I wasn't.

It wasn't long before my cell dinged, and I glanced down at the screen and giggled.

"What?" Samson asked. "What'd she say?"

"I told her to text me if things got out of hand. She said they were already out of hand, but whatever."

"I'm not sure how I feel about this," Samson said, rubbing his beard at his chin. "I mean my sister and your dad?"

"Hey. I can't think of a better person to be my new stepmom."

Samson groaned. "No. Just... no."

I wrapped my arms around his neck and kissed him. He soon took over, and I wasn't a hundred percent sure he wasn't about to bend me over the bar and fuck me right there. God knew there was a lot of that shit going down already. But he stopped short of that. I knew it wouldn't be long before he made his excuses and we headed back to our room for sex in private. Though, if I admitted it, sex in public -- at least, at a club party -- kinda turned me on. We'd have to discuss that soon.

"I love you, Lottie," he murmured between kisses. "You're always gonna be my one and only."

"I love you, too," I smiled. "We'll make this work, you know?"

"Absolutely I know," Samson said as he kissed me again. "I won't have anything else."

I kissed him again, knowing that everything would be OK. Samson was my choice. My man. God help anyone who tried to come between us.

Lawdawg (Black Reign MC 7)
Marteeka Karland

Eden: The first time I saw Grady Bassett was when Samson brought Charlotte home. Turned out my brother's woman is Grady's daughter. Naturally, the man's focus wasn't on some camgirl at a MC he had no desire to be around. When he finally does notice me, he can't see me for my position within the club -- a woman who has sex on camera for strangers. But I noticed him... and I'm a woman who knows what she wants.

Lawdawg: Eden's the most naturally sexy woman I've ever seen. Sure, I'd been worried sick about my daughter, but the second the danger to her was past, I became obsessed with Eden. I even downloaded every one of her videos. Which meant I binge watched. I'd given Samson hell for wanting my daughter when he's so much older, but now I'm in the same position. I need to let her go, to be the better man. But now I know Eden has an online stalker. He knows where she lives and who her friends are. Black Reign is compromised, so I reached out to Cain at Bones MC. This stalker is coming for Eden. But he'll have to go through me to even get close.

Chapter One

Eden

"You like it when I pinch my nipples? How about if I clamp them with these?" I dangled little clover clamps out for them to see. They were connected by a chain with a small weight in the middle. It wasn't normally my cup of tea, but Hardcase had thrown me some new stuff tonight in hopes of helping me loosen up and enjoy myself. I loved the man dearly for trying to help, but I wasn't sure anything was going to get me too excited tonight.

"Oh, yeah. That feels soooo gooood..." I crooned as I clipped the little clamps onto each nipple. It wasn't too much, but with the chain, I had control over how much pressure to put on them. It was fun, but I used it for foreplay only on cam. It took a guy to get me excited with them. Reading the messages as they came in, I noted most were enjoying the show, and I continued tugging and teasing my nipples for the rapt audience.

I worked my nipples, reading the appreciative if lewd comments and smiling as I tried to fulfill the desires of the clients watching me. I say clients because most of them tipped very well for each new scene. One of them suggested I add a bit of weight to the chain. Which I'd known would happen. Time to work the crowd.

"I could do that. But I'll need a little incentive..." Almost before I got the sentence out, several of the viewers started throwing in tips. Some as little as a couple of dollars, one or two as much as twenty. Those were my regulars. They dropped by every week to interact with me. They never failed to lead the tips so others followed suit, giving me nice sums of money.

"Thank you guys so much!" I gushed and flashed my megawatt smile as I did as requested and added weight in the form of a good-sized gem. I attached it to the chain and carefully let it settle between my breasts. I gasped, careful not to exaggerate the response too much. I wanted it to look as genuine as I could.

It took a while, but eventually, I started to get into it. Hardcase whispering dirty nothings in my ear through an earwig helped a lot. I glanced at the glass where he was monitoring everything.

"That's it, Eden," he said. "Now circle your clit a couple of times. Don't come yet." Tips continued to roll in. I'd long ago quit paying much attention to the screen. Though it was one of the reasons I had such a good following, I didn't feel like doing it today. I was too wound up about the anticipated appearance of my virtual stalker. "You look so fuckin' sexy, honey. Keep workin' your clit. Dip your fingers inside your pussy, then go back to your clit." I gasped, arching my back and thrusting my hips to my fingers.

"Yeah." I sucked in a breath before adding a third finger and pumping a couple of times. "So fucking good," I whispered.

"You're getting there, aren't you." It wasn't a question. Hardcase knew me almost as well as Iron. "So fucking hot, Eden. Just keep it up, babe. You're doing great."

I tried to lose myself in his voice, but it just wasn't happening. The closer it got to eight forty-five, the more nervous I got. Hardcase knew everything going on. He and his team monitored everything from the chats. Anyone got too bold, they shut him down.

Except for one guy. Sinner58 was his handle. Shotgun and his woman, Esther, had been working on finding out who he was, but they'd had no luck so far. At first it hadn't bothered me, but the guy had tracked down my email and phone number. I had no doubt he knew where I lived. Good thing it was in the middle of a highly secured compound full of big, rough, mean bikers.

"Come on, babe. Focus on me. On my voice. Rub your little clit again." That was Hardcase. He knew I was worried and anxious. "Do you need me or Iron to eat you out? When you come it has to be real. Can you do that on your own?"

I was cooling off. Losing the moment. "I might need some help," I whimpered. "Would you guys like to see me get my pussy eaten?"

Several more tips popped up as I glimpsed the clock. Eight forty-three. He'd be here in two minutes. I needed to get off before he arrived.

Iron was the one who came to the room. I almost sobbed in relief at his familiar face. He wasn't the man of my dreams, but he always made me feel good. This time was no exception.

He crawled on the bed with me. I knew Hardcase was moving the camera angle to get more of me and my spread legs. My wet pussy. Then Iron was between my legs, his tongue deftly flicking my clit with sure strokes.

"Fuuuuck!" I moaned long and loud. I could hear the "dings" as the tips registered on the computer. "I fucking love that!"

"You like it when I eat your pussy, baby?"

"Feels so fucking good! I want to fucking come!"

Even more "dings," signaling the crowd wanted me to come too.

"Keep going, you two," Hardcase growled in my ear. That's when I knew he was there. Sinner58. I closed my eyes, not wanting to see. Not wanting to know what was happening. I wanted to lose myself in Iron's mouth and tongue like I had so many times before. But I did look. I saw.

Little Candy... You're being naughty again.

His text gave me cold chills. I hadn't told the others he'd tracked down my phone number and email, but I was going to have to soon. I gasped and Iron rose over me, grabbing my chin and making me look directly at him.

"You focus on me," he whispered for only my ears. "Don't worry about that fuck. You worry about how hard you're gonna come on my cock, Eden."

I wanted to. I desperately wanted to, but this Sinner guy seriously freaked me out. I glanced at the screen again.

There will be consequences...

"That's it, Iron. She's done." Hardcase sounded frustrated but also angry.

"I'm sorry," I nearly sobbed. I knew it was a mistake. Sinner would think I was apologizing to him. He had in the past. But I was apologizing to Hardcase and Iron.

Iron dipped his mouth to mine. "Not your fault, baby. Can you come for me if I fuck you?"

I wanted to cry. Shaking my head, I closed my eyes. There was no way I was coming tonight. Not now.

"Can you fake it?"

I nodded.

"Ok. I'll eat your pussy. You do your thing, then we'll be done. Can you do that for me?"

"Yes," I gasped out.

Iron covered my pussy with his mouth again. We let it go on for another minute or so, then I screamed out a fake orgasm. Not my best performance, to say the least. But it got me some big tips. When one of the guys fucked me or ate me out, it always went over well. Except with Sinner58.

Once I'd finished, Hardcase wrapped it up. I burst into tears. Iron wrapped me up in his arms, awkwardly patting me. He was a wonderful fuck, but he had no idea what to do with a woman's tears.

"It's OK, sweetie. We'll get that bastard."

"I know," I sniffed. "I just... Why is this happening to me?"

"Really?" Iron pulled back, looking at me as if I'd lost my ever-loving mind. "You're a sexy, beautiful, passionate woman, honey. It's a wonder you've not been fixated on before now."

"But this guy is different. He's... I don't know. Smart. You guys can't find him and shut him down."

"We will." Hardcase opened the door and sat on the bed next to me and Iron. "We'll get this bastard, and he'll wish he'd never laid eyes on your beautiful body."

I nodded, feeling anything but sexy when there were two super protective, hot guys I knew would fuck me if I asked. Instead of using them to make myself feel better, I sat up and reached for my clothes.

"Thanks for rescuing me, Iron," I murmured softly. "I'm sorry it was a lousy show."

"It wasn't a lousy show, honey," Hardcase said. "You did good. That guy would throw anyone. Now. Why not go see what Samson's up to? I think he's back from his hunt."

"Did he find that girl? Is she OK?"

"I think so, honey," Hardcase said. "He just got back with her. The girl's father is on his way. Maybe you could show him to Fury's clinic?"

I nodded. "Yeah." Then I sighed. "Do me a solid, will you?"

"Anything, sweetheart."

"Don't tell Samson. He's got enough to worry about. I'm sure he'll find out at some point, but I think he likes this girl he went after, and I don't want him to concentrate on anything but her."

"Can't promise that, sweetheart, but I'll give it a few days. Maybe we'll get lucky, and Shotgun will nail this fucker."

"OK." It wasn't the answer I wanted, but it was all I was getting. I was lucky Hardcase agreed to wait any length of time. And I knew Samson would have a shit fit when he found out. Then a thought struck me. "Maybe I need to lay low on the camming for a while."

Hardcase sighed. "It might not be a bad idea. I didn't want to suggest it, but..."

"Yeah. I get it. Let me think about it, but don't put me on the schedule."

"OK. We can talk about it later if you want to. I'll see if Shotgun was able to find anything from this round."

"Sounds like a plan," I said, dressing before facing the two of them again. "I'm really sorry about this."

"Not your fault, baby," Iron said, sitting up. "We'll get this bastard."

I smiled. "I know." Then I was off to see our guests. I shot Samson a text, making sure he'd taken the woman to Fury's clinic. I hoped this was the woman for Samson. Lord knew he needed a good woman in his life. He was a good man. Any woman would be lucky to have someone so protective. As much as I loved my big brother, he needed someone to obsess over besides me. He tried to stay out of my life, but he was a little intense sometimes.

I jogged to the back entrance where I could hear the various vehicles and bikes rolling in. That's where I'd find this woman's father.

I wasn't exactly sure what I was expecting, but the man who jumped out of the big-ass F-450 wasn't it. He was older -- maybe mid to late forties. Though he had a large frame, it looked like it was all muscle and sinew. Not an ounce of fat. He was dressed in faded jeans and a black T-shirt that looked like it might give under the strain of his muscles.

And he looked pissed as fuck.

The Black Reign men who'd pulled in ahead of this man were headed off on their own. This guy looked around, clearly frustrated to be left with no direction. He got a determined look on his face that said he was about to tear this place apart. So I ran up to him. Out of sorts and still trembling from the appearance of my stalker, I tried my best to look like I wanted to be there helping him.

"Hey!" I called, running up to him.

"I don't have time for this horse shit," he muttered before turning to me with an exasperated expression. "What do you want?" He sounded as angry as he looked, and it kind of pissed me off because I knew exactly what he was getting at. I was a club girl -- therefore I was looking to fuck the new fish.

"Not what you think or what you'll be begging for later," I snapped. "But I will take you to your daughter. Of course, I'm just assuming you're the father of the woman my brother and his men risked their lives rescuing."

Instantly the man's full attention was on me, those glacier-green eyes boring into me like daggers. "You're Samson's sister." It wasn't a question.

"I am. Do you want to see your daughter or not?"

He gave me a once-over, his gaze drifting from my face down my body before returning to meet my eyes once more. "Yeah. You know where she is?"

I held up my phone. "We youngsters have a thing called text messaging nowadays."

His scowl deepened. "Just get the fuck on with it."

"My, my, my. So touchy." But I headed off in the direction of Fury's clinic. The walk was short, but I jogged in that direction, just to piss off the big guy. He kept pace with me easily, his long strides eating up the ground better than mine.

When we reached the clinic, I paused outside. He looked like he'd rather just burst in, but I stood in front of him, blocking his path. "You don't go into Fury's clinic without knocking unless you're recently missing a limb. Even then it's not a good idea."

"If my daughter's in there, I could give a good Goddamn," he snapped, trying to get around me again.

"Just hold up! It costs you nothing to be polite and barging inside like a bat out of hell might make whatever is going on in there worse. Just chill!"

He might have just pushed past me if Noelle, Fury's ol' lady, hadn't opened the door. She glanced at the guy before looking at me. "Your brother's fine, Eden." She looked up at our guest. "So's Charlotte, Sheriff Bassett." She stepped away from the door and motioned for us to enter. "Try not to make any loud noises or sudden movements. She's a bit traumatized."

"Sheriff, huh?" I chuckled. "Lawdawg."

He gave me a venomous look but said nothing, following Noelle inside the clinic.

"Where is she?" Sheriff Bassett asked anxiously as he stalked into the room.

I heard Charlotte whimper, and my gaze sought her out. More importantly, I needed to see how my brother was taking it. He was holding her hand, kissing the backs of her knuckles and soothing her as best he could. His tender gesture and protective posture told me all I needed to know. This was the woman for Samson.

"Hey, sister," I said, smiling gently at her as I stroked hair from her brow. "I'm Eden. Samson's sister. Welcome to the family." She looked so fragile, but I could see the steel running through her. She was holding herself together and not cringing away from the people around her she was probably meeting for the first time.

"She's not part of your family," the sheriff bit out. He looked like he wanted to throttle me and Samson both and likely would have if there hadn't been Fury and El Diablo to reckon with. El Segador was probably there also, just creeping around in the shadows like he always did. As hard as my brother protected El Diablo, El Segador -- The Reaper -- did ten times over.

"She's part of this family if she wants to be." I put myself between Lawdawg and the table where Samson sat with Charlotte.

"I need to take her home. Where she's safe." I could see he was insistent, but also that he was trying very hard to do as Noelle instructed and not create any more stress for his daughter.

I nodded. "I can understand that." When Charlotte whimpered again, I glanced at her, needing to see inside her. Did she not want to go with her dad? Had this man in some way abused her? I looked back at the sheriff and narrowed my eyes. Just to piss him off, I leaned down beside Charlotte and took her free hand in mine gently. "You don't want to go with your dad? He seems pretty capable to me."

"I just…" She looked up at her dad before closing her eyes tightly. Tears streamed down her face. "Dad has to go out sometimes. He's the sheriff. He can't be with me all the time."

That infuriated me. "Is that true? What did you plan on doing if you had to go out? Is her mom there? Who'd stay with her?"

The sheriff had the good grace to blush, standing straighter but remaining silent.

"It's not that I don't want to be home, Dad. I just… Samson promised not to leave me. I'd feel better if I was with him."

"Baby," Bassett said, taking a step forward. "You don't know these men."

"No, but I know Samson."

"You think you know him, but he's just as violent as the rest of them." I couldn't tell if Bassett hated my brother or was merely stating a fact. Thing was, I got the impression Sheriff Bassett was just as violent as the Black Reign men.

"Look, buddy," I said, taking a hostile step toward Bassett. "You might think you know who Black Reign is, but you don't. If Charlotte stays, that means she's part of this whole family. While she's here, under their protection, they will protect her with their lives. Yeah, they're all rough and wouldn't hesitate to kill a motherfucker if they had to, but they are protective to a fault. What's theirs, is protected to the death." Seriously. This guy was no better than my club. I might not be a member, but they were my family. This was my home.

"Charlotte is not theirs," Bassett said vehemently, taking a threatening step toward me. Fury and Noelle stepped between the us. "She's my daughter."

"Daddy," Charlotte whispered. "I need to stay here. I… I need it." She sounded so scared it broke my heart.

"Back off my sister, Bassett," Samson said. "If Charlotte wants to stay here at Reign, she'll have all kinds of mean men just lookin' for a reason to kill someone. Having someone threaten Charlotte would give them the excuse they want. That includes me if she's ever threatened by me. If she feels safer, what's the harm in giving her what she wants? It's not like you don't know where she's at or who has her." That was my brother. So full of confidence and protectiveness. I was so proud of him. If it was any other woman, I'd have been jealous of him dividing his attention between me and her, but I could tell by the way he looked at Charlotte she was the one. For that, I'd protect her to the death right alongside my brother.

"Besides," El Diablo said. "You wanted your shot at Wrangler. While my offer to take care of him still stands, you can't very well get the information you want from him and take care of your precious daughter at the same time." Club business wasn't my business, but this sounded like they'd discussed the topic of Wrangler already.

Bassett looked frustrated but resigned. "Fine. Yeah, I need to finish this with that fucker. I'm convinced he knows more than he's letting on, and that there are more women being held. I've been following this fucking gang for months." He scrubbed a hand over his face. "Never thought my own daughter'd be caught up in this."

"Good. You have the use of our interrogation room with Wrangler. There will be two brothers with you in that room at all times. While I don't much care what you do to the boy, I want to know exactly what you do and what information you get." He spread out his arms and grinned. "I'm just controlling that way."

"Your house," Bassett said. "Your rules."

"Then it's settled," El Diablo said with a smile. "Little Lottie will stay with Samson here at Black Reign until you're finished with your investigation or she's ready to leave."

The sheriff went to Charlotte and bent to kiss her forehead. "You need me for anything, sweetheart, call me. I'll check in on you every day."

"I love you, Daddy."

"I love you too, baby girl." He looked up at Samson with a hard stare. "I'll be back to get her when this is over."

"You can take her home when she's ready," Samson said, not backing down. "Not before."

Chapter Two

Grady
Several Days Later...

The first time I met Eden Healey, I was too worried about my daughter to really appreciate her. But she stood up to me several times that night, as well as protecting and befriending Charlotte, and that got my attention. Once that happened, I realized how beautiful and appealing she truly was.

She was slight but curvy, with generous breasts and hips. She was stunningly beautiful with her curly, dark auburn hair and dark brown eyes and sweet-as-sin smile. Literally the girl next door. And she wasn't much older than my daughter. If at all. For the first time since my wife died, I found myself seriously turned on by a woman.

After I got home, she was all I could think about. Her smile. The way she stood between me and Charlotte. The fierce look in her eyes as she protected my daughter. It was all more than I could let go.

Even as I was "questioning" that scum, Wrangler, I was looking into little Eden. She might look innocent, but she was far from it. I wasn't sure how I felt about what I found, but I damned sure researched it. Thoroughly.

Turned out Eden wasn't only a club girl at Black Reign, but she worked as a cam girl for them, going under the handle OI8CandyCam. So I did what any self-respecting investigator would do. I subscribed to the service and downloaded every single video she had posted.

That was both a blessing and a curse. I got to see every gorgeous inch of a woman I was fast becoming obsessed with, but I had to watch her fuck other guys.

It was torture. It was the sweetest pleasure. I lost count of the number of times I'd come watching her come.

I was so fucked.

Sitting at home at my desk in the dark, I watched her now. It was a live feed, and it felt erotic to know exactly what she was doing at this very moment. I wasn't exactly trying to be subtle about perving on her either. I'd used the handle she'd given me inadvertently the day we met. Lawdawg. If she noticed, she didn't mention it. She probably wouldn't, given she was a professional. I grinned as I thought about her calling me out when I met up with her later. And I knew absolutely I would meet her again. I talked to her nearly every day, checking up on Charlotte. That was because Eden was always with Charlotte. Sometimes even if Samson was with her. And, let's face it, I would much rather talk to Eden than that prick Samson.

"You like that, huh?" she purred as one guy commented on how sexy her little cunt looked with her fingers swirling around it wet with her juices. It made me want to punch the motherfucker, but he had a point. "You like it when I play with my pussy?"

A chorus of "yes," and "YES," and "FUCK YES!" popped up on the chat screen as she grinned.

"So greedy," she tsked. "If you want more… you know what I need."

The chat screen went crazy with twenty or thirty guys tossing tips her way. She grinned and continued her little tease, using a dildo on herself. She moaned and squirmed like she was really having a good time. The camera had two different angles, and whoever was operating it did a superb job of moving the angle from her cunt to her face.

Just as she was ready to come, I noticed names

I'd seen on several of her videos start to put in tips. Obviously, they were preparing for her to come. It didn't take long. She screamed out her orgasm, and the production guy split the screen to show both angles. I could clearly see the ecstasy on her face and the way her cunt spasmed and twitched as she came around the toy. She'd really come for the camera and all the people watching. That just made me hard as fuck.

I took out my dick and squeezed it, stroking once. My fucking brain went straight to a place where Eden's soft palm was wrapped around my dick and pumping it, begging for my cum. It took all of three pumps before I shot my load all over my pants. I grunted loudly, my head falling back on my chair as I relished the release of pressure to my dick. Breathing heavily, I closed my eyes and went limp for several seconds, trying to get a grip on my raging libido. God knew it had been a long fucking time since I'd wanted a woman this hard. I couldn't seem to get Eden out of my mind!

When she signed off, I quickly pulled up another video of her. This one I'd downloaded into my collection. It had her fucking another guy. I thought it was the man called Iron from Black Reign. I gritted my teeth, jealousy seething inside me even as my dick quickly hardened again. I lasted a little longer this time, but before I finally called it a night, I'd come three fucking times. I hadn't done that since I was a fucking teenager! What was this girl doing to me?

"Fuck," I bit out. "Just fuck it all."

As if I'd conjured her, my phone rang. Eden. Fuck. Had it not been for Charlotte, there's no way I would have answered that call. Not fresh off coming after watching Eden's videos. But I couldn't take the chance, even to save my pride.

"Yeah, Eden. Everything OK?"

"Well, someone's surly," she said with an abundance of sass. "Charlotte's fine. I just called to thank you for the bank. I might even be able to skip Friday's show because of the tips you sent my way.

Of *course*, she saw the handle. "I have no idea what you're talking about."

"Just tell me which part you liked best. The part where I showed my new piercing? Or the part where I showed you how to make me come with it?"

"One of these days, Eden, you're gonna push me too far."

"Oh, yeah? What's gonna happen then?"

I ground my teeth in frustration. When she finally made me snap, I was taking her over my knee and spanking her sweet ass. "Just tell me about Charlotte. I can't get a straight answer outa Samson because he just wants in her panties. You're a pain in my ass, but I know you care about my daughter." That usually made Eden sober up. She seemed to delight in telling me how wonderfully Charlotte was settling in. It wasn't that I begrudged her this happiness, I just worried Samson would take advantage of her in a fragile state. Samson was too much like me to ever be what Lottie needed. He'd make her reliant on him, then use her until he got tired of her. Charlotte was too tender-hearted to survive a man like that for long.

Eden sighed. "You know she's doing fine. She's healing nicely and smiles so much more often. I promise you, Grady, she's really doing well. And Samson is taking good care of her. When he can't be with her -- and that isn't often -- he has me come stay with her. He's keeping his promise to her. And you."

I grunted my approval. "Good."

"But if you're hoping I'll warn her off Samson,

you can set your hopes on something else. Lottie makes him happy when no one else ever has. You're barking up the wrong tree, hoss. Those two belong together."

I'd have to think about that one. I couldn't deny Lottie sounded happier than I could ever remember her sounding. But was I ready to give her up to a fucking biker who was closer to my age than hers? Not on your fucking life.

And so it continued. I kept stalking Eden. She kept teasing me about it. I learned to live with my baby girl taking on a biker. Hard lessons, all of them.

Then one day I got a direct message from a guy calling himself Sinner58.

Back off, Lawdawg. Or I'll make sure you regret it.

It was followed by a picture of me in uniform outside the courthouse in Glades County, and immediately after, one of Charlotte in front of the Black Reign compound as she left with Eden *this morning*. I knew it was this morning because I recognized both outfits the girls were wearing. Lottie had on a pale yellow sundress that made her look like a cross between an angel and a sex kitten (which made me cringe), and Eden wore leather shorts and a leather halter with thigh-high stiletto-heeled boots. I wasn't comfortable with either woman dressed like that, but knew better than to say anything. Now, my protective instincts were on full alert. First person I wanted to call? Fucking Samson. Unfortunately, I'm a fucking dumbass who didn't want the other man's number. Any beef I had with him I'd take straight to that El Diablo character himself. Or the fucking police in Lake Worth. The only person I could get hold of with any connection to that fucking club was Vincent Black at the DA's office.

"You need to tell Samson to lock down Lottie and Eden," I said as I prepared to leave, slamming closed the lid to my laptop.

"Why?" The other man snapped his question in a clipped, sharp voice.

"I just got a warning from one of Eden's cam show followers to back off her. The bastard sent me a picture of Eden and Lottie he'd taken just this morning."

"The fuck?"

"They're in danger."

"Yeah, no shit. I'll take care of this." The other man now sounded distracted. Like he had already started working on a plan. Or maybe he was blowing me off.

"You better," I bit out. "Anything happens to either woman before I get there, I'll burn that whole Goddamned compound to the fuckin' ground!"

There was no answer because the line went dead. Immediately, I called Eden. I preferred to deal with her club or her brother on this, but she needed to know she was in danger.

She answered on the first ring. "Hey there, Lawdawg. How's it hangin'?" She hiccuped slightly at the end and giggled.

"Are you... are you drunk?"

"Well, yeah. It's a party, you know. We're all drunk."

"Great," I muttered. "Just fuckin' great." I scrubbed a hand over my face but continued. "Listen to me, Eden. Go to Samson. You're in danger. There's a guy stalking you."

"Sinner58? Yeah. I know. He's running off all my good followers." She sounded like she was pouting.

"You knew about this?" Anger was starting to

build inside me. Anger. Aggression. I wanted to take her over my knee and paddle her like the child she was.

"Of course, I knew! He's been bullying my regulars for weeks. It's just that it must have stepped up in the last few days, because my followers are leaving now instead of merely waiting until the next show."

"Did you tell anyone?"

"Nope." No further explanation.

"Of course, you didn't." I let out an exasperated breath. "Look. Just stay put. This guy knows where you are and how to get to you. I'm headed that way."

"Oh, you are, huh?"

"Eden..." I tried to inject as much warning as I could. Anyone else would have tripped all over themselves to do his bidding. Eden? Not so much.

"What do you plan on doing when you get here?"

"I'm lockin' that place down with you in it!"

"Oh, really?"

"I don't have time to argue with you, Eden," I snapped, beginning to get really angry now. Well, angry but more frustrated. She wasn't taking this seriously at all. Hadn't in all the time she knew about it.

"You don't?" I sensed a trap but had no idea what it might be. "Well, what if I did this..." There was a pause before my phone signaled I had a text. I pulled it up and there was a selfie of Eden. Her exquisite tits on fine display. "Or this." The next image she sent had a man sucking at one of those tits. Something inside me just... snapped. I felt like something inside my head that was primitive and territorial roared to the front and demanded I claim that woman. She was mine. No one else's. It didn't seem to matter she was young enough to be my daughter or that my late wife was probably rolling over in her grave because of the girl's age. I needed her and had every intention of taking her with me. I could tell myself it was to keep her safe, but the pure and simple fact was, I just fucking wanted her.

"Goddammit, Eden! When I get there, I'm gonna paddle your ass."

"Not what I want you to do with my ass, baby," she purred. "Now, if you wanna fuck my ass, we might be able to negotiate on that one." The little bitch had been tormenting me since the night Samson and I had fought. It was coming to a head tonight.

With a vicious oath, I headed out to my own bike. The Harley Davidson FDXR114 was my pride and joy. One I kept locked up in the garage and never took out. But it would get me there faster than anything. Even my cruiser would struggle to go faster. Not because it wasn't as powerful, but because it was less maneuverable. I could -- and did -- zigzag through traffic like the hounds of hell were after me. Straight to the Black Reign compound. Surprisingly, the guards at the gate let me in, opening the door before I even slowed.

Once inside, I drove straight to the front fucking door before shutting it down and swinging my leg over the side, dismounting.

"Dude, nice ride!" The guy who spoke looked young. Early twenties, maybe. He ran to catch up with me. The gate was only a couple hundred feet from the main building, so he didn't have far to go. I would've avoided the bastard altogether, but there were two more guys blocking my way. Probably belatedly alerted by dumbass here.

"Where's Samson?" I demanded without preamble.

"In a meeting with El Diablo, I think." When I started inside, they tried to stop me, but I kept moving.

"Hey! You can't go in there!" one of the other guys yelled. "That's club property." He made the mistake of getting too close, and I proceeded to beat the piss outa the little fuck in a spray of blood and spit. He didn't deserve it. He just happened to be the first person I was able to take out my frustration on. I was sure I'd feel bad about it later, but really. He let me in. Probably because he had a hard-on for my bike. That was inexcusable, especially when my daughter and Eden were in danger.

I heard a gun being cocked an instant before the cold steel of the barrel was pressed against the base of my skull.

"Enough," the voice said. Deep and gravelly and laced with anger. "You don't get to beat a prospect inside our club." I turned my head to see the one they called Shadow. He wasn't officially a member of this club -- from what I understood he was a member of a club in Kentucky -- but his expression was unyielding.

"He let me in without knowing who I was. He gonna let anyone in with a bitchin' bike?"

Shadow raised an eyebrow and glanced at the man I had pinned beneath me. He looked back at the gate to see it swinging shut, then back to the prospect, scowling. "Have at him, then."

"Shadow!" The prospect squeaked when I raised my hand to start pounding him again, but I only hit him once more. It was hard enough to knock his ass out, but still. Then I slapped him several times to get him to moan and open his eyes.

"You had one job, motherfucker," Shadow said

matter-of-factly. "Watch the fuckin' gate."

"I was watchin' it!" the man whined. "But that's a fuckin' sweet bike!"

"That's it," I said. "Motherfucker's having a fatal accident right here."

That all changed the second my phone went off again. This pic was one of her sweet, bare little pussy. Nothing I hadn't already seen, but she'd sent this picture directly to me. I didn't ask for it. I wouldn't have taken it if she'd asked if I'd wanted it. But now that I had it, it belonged to me. That was followed by a series of photos she'd obviously put together ahead of time. Her eating another woman out. Two men sucking her tits. Eden wearing nipple clamps that dangled with sparkling gems. What I was pretty sure was her ass with a jeweled anal plug sparkling between her luscious cheeks.

I hit my limit.

"Fuck," I bit out as I pocketed my phone. "That is *enough.*"

I stalked to the entrance of the clubhouse. I could hear the party before I even got to the door. Once there, I thrust it open so hard, it bounced off the wall, and I had to shove it back again. The group of men hollered out a greeting. Someone tossed me a beer, which I caught in one hand. Normally, I'd have popped the top and guzzled it. Lord knew I needed it. Instead, I set it down as I scanned the room.

I caught a hit of her musical laughter before I actually saw her. A second later, I found her. Her head was thrown back in her merriment while that mane of dark hair fluttered around her naked torso. The two men helping her pose for lewd selfies spotted me before she did and, with a kiss to her cheek, promptly abandoned her. Out of the corner of my eye, I saw Iron.

He looked like he might come to her aid but backed off. Probably when he saw the expression on my face. I knew I had bared my teeth. I could only imagine how I looked. I felt feral. Out of control.

"Oh, shit. You've had it now, Eden." I recognized Charlotte's voice, but even that couldn't shake me out of the madness. Eden, the little minx, finally saw me coming and tucked her phone into her back pocket. She gave me a little smirk as she picked up her bottle of beer and took a heavy pull. She'd just set the bottle down when I reached her. I couldn't form words. Her perky little tits were on full display, and my mouth watered for them.

Personally, I thought I showed restraint by not shoving her face-first across the bar and fucking her right on the spot. That was me being courteous. Instead, I scooped her up over my shoulder, swatting her ass for good measure.

"You fucking bastard! Put me down!"

I didn't respond, just swatted her ass again as I scanned the bar for the one man who could possibly stop me. Samson met my gaze with a hard one of his own. He shook his head slightly, but sighed in resignation, nodding to me once. Then I shifted my gaze to find Charlotte. As expected, she wasn't far from Samson. I saw her phone sitting on the bar and pointed to it. If she wanted to check on Eden, she could do it by phone.

Immediately, Lottie picked up her phone and sent off a fast text. When Eden's phone buzzed from her back pocket, I dug it out of her shorts and handed it to her. She screeched and hit me in the head with it to express her displeasure. So, I spanked her ass again. Yeah. I was gonna enjoy this more than words could express.

I had no idea what Lottie texted Eden, but Eden muttered something foul and sent her own text before hitting me in the head again with her phone.

"Do it again, I'll wallop your ass right here," I said as I marched out of the compound with her still over my shoulder.

"Put me down! I'm naked!"

"Are not. You got shorts on," I said, acutely aware she had shorts on because I wanted a taste of the bare pussy she'd shown me.

I set her down next to my bike and shrugged out of my jacket. She snatched it out of my hand and put it on with snappish movements. "Fucker."

"Get on the fuckin' bike."

"Only reason I am is because it's a bitchin' bike." She climbed on the back, careful of the pipes like she'd climbed on the back of one a thousand times.

I scowled at her as I climbed on and revved the engine. "Yeah. It is a bitchin' bike."

The ride back to my home took far less time than it should have. I pushed the bike as much as I dared because the faster I went, the more Eden seemed to like it. And fuck me if I could deny her this pleasure. Once home, however, I hardened my heart. I was getting her out of here. With Eden away, it would buy Black Reign some time to find this stalker and disappear him.

When we pulled into my driveway, I ushered her into the garage and my Ford F-350. "Stay put," I said, pointing a finger at her.

"What are you doing?"

"Loadin' my bike. Ain't leavin' it here. Those bastards from your club would likely steal it and go for joy rides."

"Where do you think you're taking me?"

I gave her a hard look, hoping she saw just how

determined I was to get her out of here. "We're going to Kentucky. I've contacted the Bones president, Cain. He and I are old friends."

"Why are we going to Kentucky?" The girl looked genuinely confused. Like she didn't understand the gravity of the situation. It pissed me off something fierce.

"Don't you understand the gravity of the situation? You have a stalker. He knows where you live. He knows who your friends are. It's only a matter of time before he tries to take what he wants. Until we figure out who this bastard is, I'm taking you somewhere you're safe."

"Other than running off my followers and high tippers, he's harmless." Her gaze darted away from mine. "Mostly." Yeah. She knew better. Probably arguing because I'd pulled her ass out of the situation without consulting her. And she continued to spout nonsense.

"You don't know that. And I really don't think he's so harmless. I think he'll make a play to kidnap you soon."

"Based on…"

"Twenty fucking years' experience in law enforcement. Now shut the fuckin' door and sit tight until I load the bike on the trailer and hook up."

Chapter Three

Eden

I thought about flipping Grady off and making a run for it, but why? I mean, he'd just hauled me out over his shoulder and absconded with me. Was I freaked out by the stalker dude? Kinda. But it was more that I was afraid he'd run off all my followers. If that happened, I'd have to start finding new ways to bring in money for the club, and I really liked camming.

Grady got in and shoved a T-shirt at me while he started the truck. Pulling it out of the garage and backing it up to the enclosed trailer, he hooked up with practiced ease. I assumed his precious bike was in there. I was glad because I really wanted to ride with him again. While I'd lived with Black Reign for a long time, the only time I'd ridden on the back of someone's bike had been when Samson offered. As a rule, unless it was an emergency, the only woman on the back of a man's bike was his woman. And I was nobody's woman.

Once he'd finished hooking up the trailer and making sure everything was secure, Grady slid behind the wheel and slammed the door to the truck.

"You know, if you're taking me all the way to Kentucky, don't you think I should have packed some clothes?"

"You can pick up some once we get there. I explained to Cain what's goin' on, and he said his ol' lady, Angel, will have you a few things when we get there."

"I'd rather have my own stuff," I grumbled, not really put out, but needing to make a proper fuss.

"Tough shit. If you'd bothered to tell anyone

about this, you might've had a controlled exit." He pulled out onto the road and started us on our way.

"Should be a fun trip," I said, grinning at him. "We'll have all night and part of the day." I grinned. "Unless you plan on stopping. If we get a motel, I want a nice one with thick walls. That way, when I make you bellow to the rafters, no one will call the cops."

"No," he said in a clipped tone. "Don't even think it, because that's not happening."

"Oh? So, you like living dangerously." I tapped my chin thoughtfully. "I guess it makes sense. As a sheriff, you'd have some pull with local law enforcement, I guess." I shrugged. "Just as well. I like knowing that everyone could hear you when we fucked."

"Eden," he said, a warning note in his voice. "Just get all those thoughts of sex outta your head. I'm not here to fuck you. It's not happening."

I giggled. "We'll see."

We passed the next several hours in silence. Apparently, Sheriff Grady Barrett did *not* believe in the radio. Or small talk. Or anything that took his attention away from the road, really. Yeah. That was just waving a red flag in my face.

"Did you enjoy my little photo documentary of all the fun I had tonight?" The truck lurched, and Grady gritted his teeth. Yeah. I'd hit a nerve. He probably loved *and* hated it.

"Now's not the time, Eden," he growled.

"Well, when is? 'Cause I wanna talk about it." I smiled brightly at him. The sun was setting and the light fading, but when he glanced at me, throwing an appropriately menacing scowl in my direction, I knew he could see my expression.

"Never. And you'll erase those photos from your

phone. You're not to send them to anyone. Shit goes up on the Internet, it's forever. One day you'll thank me for this."

I laughed merrily, absently squeezing one tit through the jacket he'd given me. I'm sure he completely forgot to make sure I'd actually put on the T-shirt. When I got "too warm" and had to take the jacket off, I could taunt him with the fact that I'd asked nicely to stop back by the clubhouse and get some clothes.

"Right. You do know my image is up all over the Internet. Right? I mean, me playing with myself, fucking my pussy with toys. Me fucking guys. Coming on cam…" I let my voice trail off, watching intently as his jaw clenched and his hands tightened on the wheel at two and ten. He was such a Goody-Two-shoes! It was also hard to miss his cock stirring behind his jeans.

"Doesn't mean you should let personal photos get out. They aren't…" He fumbled for a word. "In the same setting."

I grinned, leaning on the console arm rest between us. "I bet you got excited looking at me. Didn't you." I didn't phrase it as a question. It was obvious. Painfully so for him given how the bulge in his pants had grown.

When he didn't answer, I slowly reached out, sliding my hand over his thigh to settle over his cock, and squeezed. He jerked. Both in the seat and beneath my palm, but he didn't take his hands from the wheel.

"Don't," he said, his nostrils flaring, his face hard and predatory.

Naturally, I ignored him, continuing to squeeze and rub his crotch. It took all of a minute before he groaned and thrust his hips at my hands subtly. He stilled immediately, but the damage was done.

I unbuttoned his jeans, then slid the zipper down. I could have rolled my eyes if I hadn't been so hungry for the man. Of course, he had on tighty-whities. Besides that, he was sex on a stick and forbidden. Catnip to a girl like me.

Not wanting to give him time to protest, I pulled his cock out and let it spring to life. Straight and proud and throbbing in my palm, Grady was magnificent. Thick, veiny, and long, his cock was beautiful and made my mouth water, longing to taste it.

Without waiting, afraid he'd call a halt if I hesitated too long, I flipped up the center console and lay down to wiggle my head under Grady's arms and engulf his cock.

"Mother fuck!" Grady's words exploded from his throat in a gasp. One hand left the steering wheel and gripped my head. I wasn't sure if he intended to pull me off him or not, but his fingers tunneled into my hair and gripped almost painfully. I sucked until he pulled my head up slowly. I thought he might pull me off him, but instead, he pushed me back down. The breath exploded from his lungs, and he gave a sharp cry.

"Goddammit! Eden!"

"Mmmmm…"

I couldn't help but grin. He tasted delicious. The little shot of pre-cum I got when he pushed me back down, his cock head grazing my tongue lightly, was like a hit of ambrosia. I wanted this. Wanted his cum in my mouth, and I was willing to work for it no matter how hard I had to.

Pumping his length with my hand, I continued to suck him, bobbing my head up and down as much as I could. Though I led the dance, Grady controlled me. Well, as much as he was able to. His fist tightened in my hair reflexively, but he seemed unable to actually pull me off him. When he needed me to slow down, he pulled me back but didn't let his cock slip out of my mouth completely.

"What the fuck are you doing to me?" His question was bitten out between clenched teeth. I got the feeling it was a musing more than an actual question. The thought that I'd brought him to this state so quickly was heady. Grady Bassett was just as big a badass as the men of Black Reign. But in that moment, I decided he was my badass.

"Stop," Grady barked out. Yeah. That wasn't happening. "I said stop, Eden!" His voice was gruffer than I'd ever heard him. His fingers were bunched tightly in my hair and, though he was telling me to stop, he kept urging me to move on him.

It must have taken a force of will, but he finally let me up. Not because I pushed away from him. He just suddenly let go of my hair so I could comply with him.

"You're not enjoying yourself?" I looked up at him, still stroking his cock with my hand. He was slowing down, pulling the truck off to the side of the road. He didn't answer me, but the second he stopped, he slammed the gear shift into park and shoved me backward. My upper body landed against the door, though not hard. The next thing I knew, he was yanking my shorts and panties over my hips and diving between my legs.

"Little witch," he hissed against my sex. "Gonna eat you alive." That voice was the biggest turn-on in the world. Growly. Gruff. He didn't pull my shorts off. Just shoved my legs to my chest and latched on to my sex with his mouth.

"Fuck! Grady!" The man had a wicked tongue! I was turned on from sucking his dick, but this was madness! The things he was doing with his teeth and lips and tongue drove me up quicker than I'd ever thought possible. I hadn't even kissed the man, for crying out loud! "Gonna fucking come!"

He pulled back slightly, only to smack my pussy with the flat of his hand. "Don't you fuckin' dare! You hold off until I tell you."

Was he kidding? Hold back? I'd spent the last several months of my life trying to reach the point where I needed to come. Working the cam rooms needed to be authentic. Hardcase taught us all that you didn't fake orgasms if you could help it. He did everything he could to get each of us there, and we embraced it. Now Grady wanted me to hold off?

"Can't!" I screamed as the orgasm washed over me. Grady covered my pussy with his mouth and caught my cream as the most intense orgasm of my life crashed through me. It happened so fast, I barely had time to process I was there when my whole body seized, and I let go.

"Fuck," he swore, still licking and sucking my cunt. "So fuckin' sweet." Grady drew out my orgasm expertly until I finally went limp beneath his touch. Once I was passive beneath him, panting for breath, he raised his head and kissed my mound, then my flat belly. "Fuck."

He pulled my shorts back into place, and I sat up. Immediately, I went back to his cock. His breath was as heavy as mine, his cock pulsing in my mouth as I continued what I'd started.

Grady let his head fall back on the seat as he groaned. His hands were in my hair, guiding me, urging me on. Over and over he kept hissing out, "Fuck, fuck, fuck," as I worked him. He throbbed in my mouth, pulsing and moving, his cock telling me he was almost there when I knew Grady the man never could.

I took him deep and hummed around him like I was eating my favorite treat. It was all Grady needed. With a brutal yell, he let go a stream of cum into my mouth, emptying his balls like he hadn't come in forever. I squealed around him, catching everything he had to give me in the haven of my mouth. He was salty sweet on my tongue, and I craved the taste of him, as well as his unabashed responses. To me, there was nothing sexier than a man yelling in the throes of passion. Grady gave that to me in spades.

Once he'd settled down, his breath still coming in little pants, I looked up at him. He had this adorable shell-shocked expression on his face, like he couldn't believe what had just happened. Little beads of sweat dotted his forehead and upper lip. He looked like a man who'd just thoroughly had his mind blown.

The second he realized what had happened, he scowled at me, stuffing his dick back in his pants and fastening them. I curled up in the passenger's seat where I'd been sitting. I know there was a satisfied smirk on my face, but I couldn't seem to help myself. Grady gave me a look like he thought I was the devil incarnate. Which only made me grin bigger. Truth was, I loved that I'd just blown his mind.

"You need to watch yourself, Eden," he snapped. "It's behavior like this that caused you problems in the first Goddamned place."

That took me aback. "Excuse me? What's my behavior got to do with it?"

"Every fucking thing!" he roared, then scrubbed his hand over his face. "It's this kind of thing that earned you a stalker. What exactly were you planning on doing about him, anyway?"

Had Grady slapped me, he couldn't have surprised me more. "So, the stalker is my own fault? Seriously?"

"You put yourself out there on the Internet, fucking anyone who comes along, and you don't expect every psycho to want a piece of the action?"

"You know what? Fuck you, *Lawdawg*," I spat the nickname I knew he hated. "I am not ashamed of anything I've done to help my club! I didn't fuck just anyone who came along. It was fucking business! I got pleasure, and so did the brothers fucking me, but I knew ahead of time who was coming in to help out and what to expect. Besides, it's none of your Goddamned business! I don't have to justify myself to you!"

"Look," he said. I could see he thought he was trying to be reasonable in an unreasonable situation. "We'll talk about this when you're sober."

"I'm not drunk! What the fuck, Grady?"

"You may not be drunk, but I'm sure you're still tipsy. You wouldn't be acting this way, throwing yourself at me, if you weren't buzzed."

"You saying I don't know my own mind? That I'd just fuck a guy because I was drunk and horny?"

He shrugged before putting the truck in gear and heading back out onto the road. He'd chosen to take the back roads instead of the interstate. Probably in case we were being followed. It was easier to spot a tail when not in a high-traffic area. "I'm just saying you wouldn't be all over me like this if you were sober. You'd look for a man closer to your age with more in common than being in the same enclosed space."

"I'm not ashamed for loving sex, Grady. I'm not ashamed of the things I've done in the past or will likely do in the future. I'm a woman who loves sex.

You don't like it? Fuck you." Why the fuck was there a sharp pain in my chest over this? This son of a bitch meant nothing to me but a good time.

He was silent for a long while. Though on the state roads instead of the interstate, the current road we were on was lit by streetlamps every so often. I could see his jaw clenched as he continued on. His forearms bulged with tension where he gripped the wheel.

"Just try to get some sleep. It's going to be a long night."

Somewhere in the back of my mind, I put together that Grady was probably mad at himself for what he saw as taking advantage of me. If he thought I was drunk, that was likely how he saw the situation. It didn't make it hurt any less. With a sigh, I turned to look out my window.

He was right about one thing, though. I was still buzzing. I'd have still made a move on him even if I was stone-cold sober, though. It was what I'd been leading up to for days. It might have started out as a personal joke designed to help Grady accept his daughter being with Samson, but it had become something more to me. Not only was Grady over-the-top protective, but he was sexy as sin. I wanted his intensity focused on me. Wanted that protection for myself because he saw me as something more than an obligation. If that made me a bad person, so be it. The only problem was, I'd decided I kind of wanted him for my own. It would never happen. Didn't mean I couldn't dream about it.

Trying to ignore Grady, I turned my face away from him and stared out the window at the lights speeding by. If I had a few tears, so be it.

But a few tears turned into many. Thankfully, I

managed to keep it to a slow leak instead of the full-on sobbing I wanted to do. It wasn't like it mattered. It was my own damn fault for thinking anyone outside of Black Reign would understand, anyway.

* * *

Grady

We stopped at a little bed and breakfast just as dawn was breaking. I didn't want to travel during the day, and I knew the people who owned it. They'd have a place I could hide my truck and trailer and would let me pay cash for the room. I didn't say anything to Eden when I got out to check in. Just left her in the truck. The girl hadn't moved since our fight. I suspected she was more upset than I realized when she didn't make a move to get out or look at me when I stopped. I even paused for a moment when I opened the door, prepared to tell her to stay put. She said nothing.

"I'll be right back." Still she said nothing, but she didn't look like she was making a break for it, so I refrained from telling her to stay in the truck. Yeah. I knew I'd been an asshole. Hell, I didn't care about her past adventures other than the fact that I hadn't been involved. And why would I have been? She didn't know me any more than I knew her.

I secured a small room for us with one bed. I wasn't taking a chance of her bugging out on me while I slept, so I was insisting she sleep in the same room with me. Probably in the same bed. Though I was a light sleeper, I had the feeling Eden was wiley when she needed to be, and she'd slip right out of the room the moment she knew I was asleep.

I returned to the truck and parked it where it was hidden from prying eyes. "Come on," I said. "Got us a room."

She sniffed, turning her face away and swiping at her eyes quickly. Shoving open the door, she hopped down out of my jacked-up ride and slammed the door shut. She didn't look at me so much as she looked through me, just waiting patiently for me to lead the way. I wanted to take her hand but didn't dare. If I touched her again, I wasn't sure I could restrain myself. Already I was rethinking the single room. The only thing that prevented me from changing my mind was knowing she'd run off if I gave her half a chance.

I unlocked the door and stepped back to let Eden go in first. She still didn't look at me. Instead, she went straight to the bathroom and locked the door.

Once I locked everything up and pulled the drapes closed, I sat on the edge of the bed and waited, listening for any noise coming from the bathroom. The shower was going but other than that I didn't hear a sound. It wasn't long before the shower stopped and I could hear her moving around. I sat there, waiting patiently, feeling more guilty for my earlier outburst than I wanted to admit. I didn't care if she slept with a hundred different men. Not really. OK, so I *cared*. I certainly didn't like thinking about her with other men. But it didn't really matter. Not in the grand scheme of things. I was more concerned with what happened next. Now that I'd had a taste of her, I was certain I'd want more. To say I cared only meant I didn't want her to fuck anyone else other than me from here on out, and I wasn't certain how I felt about that.

She came out of the bathroom, a towel wrapped around her. The big, fluffy thing covered her from armpits to knees in terrycloth. Her hair was wrapped up tightly as well. Eden glanced at me as she passed but said nothing. She looked... young. Vulnerable.

And more sexy than I was comfortable with. The moment I saw her, I knew I was damned to the deepest pits of hell, because the brief taste I'd had of her wasn't going to be enough. I wanted Eden with every breath in my body.

The little bed and breakfast had a vanity kit sitting in a little nook beside the bathroom. There was a brush, comb, and a hairdryer on the counter. Eden muttered a soft, "Bathroom's yours," before picking up the comb and detangling her hair.

I stood transfixed for a long time. Just watching her pull the comb through the long tresses was somehow erotic to the extreme. Her face was expressionless, but I could see the hurt there. The way she was holding herself together by a single thread.

The next thing I knew, I was standing right behind her. Eden remained focused on her own reflection, ignoring me as completely as if I weren't even there. I was reminded of an Alice Cooper song, which only emphasized the age disparity between us. I doubt this young woman even knew who Alice Cooper was, let alone one of his sexiest songs. Her lips were venomous poison. And I wasn't certain if I wanted to break the chains she'd wrapped me up in.

When I set my hands gently on her shoulders, she closed her eyes. One tear tracked down her cheek…

And I was done.

I sank to my knees, turning her on the stool where she sat at the vanity so that she faced me. "You're so lovely, Eden," I murmured. I hadn't meant to say anything, but faced with the ethereal vision in front of me, I couldn't stop the words. "I was out of line before. Upset that I let you get to me when I should be protecting you from fuckers like me."

"It's fine." Her voice was small, and she looked down at her lap, not resisting me but not participating either. With a sigh, I took the comb from her hand and set it aside. I reached for the brush and stood, turning her back to face the mirror as I did. She met my gaze in the mirror before lowering her gaze once more. Yeah. I'd hurt her bad.

With long, even strokes, I brought the brush through her hair over and over. The long, damp tresses felt like silk as they slid over my fingers. I kept this up for a long while, hoping she'd relax into my touch. It was the least I could do after how badly my words had hurt her.

"You're so much more than you seem on the surface, Eden. You went out of your way to make my daughter feel welcomed and safe when she came to your club. I want you to know I appreciate that." She nodded her thanks, but only glanced up at me as if she were surprised at the admission. "What I said before," I intentionally brought us back to my earlier belittling of her. "It was as inexcusable as it was wrong. This situation is in no way your fault." I waited until she met my gaze in the mirror. There was skepticism in her gaze as well as a healthy dose of hurt.

"I happen to be a woman who loves sex, Grady. I'm never going to apologize for that, or for the way I've lived my life. I learned when my parents died that life was too short to conform to other people's ideas of what was right and wrong."

"And you're right to live that way. I let things get out of hand and was angry at myself."

She started. "Because of what I did? That I pushed you into a sexual situation that you didn't want?"

"No, honey. Because I should be protecting you

- 152 -

from fuckin' perverts like me." That must have been the exact wrong thing to say because she pushed back from the table and stood abruptly, a scowl on her face. It didn't mask the tears glistening in her eyes, though.

"So you're a pervert because you ate me out in a truck on the side of the fucking highway," she snapped. "Why does it always have to be perverted when a woman wants to do something adventurous with a hot guy?" She muttered her question, but it seemed rhetorical, because she waved her hand in the air as she marched away from me to where she'd laid the T-shirt I'd given her earlier. Naturally I followed. "Don't worry, Mr. High and Mighty. I won't upset your delicate sensibilities with an offer of sex again, since you find it so distasteful."

I stopped her march as well as her tirade by gripping her shoulders in my big hands. "Stop, Eden. Just... stop. That's not what I meant."

She snorted but looked back over her shoulder. "Then just what did you mean exactly?"

"That a man my age shouldn't be taking advantage of a woman your age."

Eden just rolled her eyes as she turned to face me. "As if you're that good. No one takes advantage of me, Grady. I'm an experienced woman who knows what she wants. If I didn't want to fuck you, I wouldn't have tried."

When she would have shrugged me off, I tightened my grip on her. "Yeah? And what if I decided I wanted to keep you? What if it wasn't just a fuck I was after, huh?"

"You don't want that," she said with a confident air, waving away my words with one elegant hand. "You hate me. Not only that, you hate that your daughter ended up with my brother. If anything, I'd think you'd go along with me just to get back at Samson. And, to tell you the truth, I ain't worried about that at all."

"Oh?"

"No. You ain't the type of man who'd do that. Not with an innocent person. Not even one you dislike. You might throw another woman your daughter's age at Samson just to see if he'd bite, but you'd never go after his sister, who is only a year or two older than your daughter, just to get back at him."

"I don't hate you, Eden. Not at all. I simply know my limitations, and there is no way under the sun I can resist you."

She looked so adorably confused, I had to bite my lip to keep from grinning. Slowly, I let my hands slide down to her towel. It was held in place with one end tucked between her breasts, and I pulled it free. The terrycloth fluttered to the floor to puddle at her feet, and Eden stood gloriously naked before me. Instead of looking shy or unsure of herself, she lifted her chin defiantly and shoved her shoulders back. Her breasts, those glorious, beautiful tits, were thrust out in offering to me. Eden raised one eyebrow as if to ask me what the fuck I was gonna do now. I honestly had no idea. Not until I found myself reaching for one nipple, covering it with the center of my palm.

My eyes closed in bliss at the satiny soft feel of her skin. My fingers brushed the side of her rib cage, and I stroked little caresses where they landed. Her nipple pebbled under my palm, and her lips parted. I could tell she tried to suppress her reaction, and it made a white-hot flash of anger surge through me. My grip on her body tightened, my fingers digging into her side.

"Don't... do that," I bit out, unsure how to

verbalize what I needed. The blood in my brain seemed to have made a beeline south.

"Do what?" Brow knit in confusion.

"Hide from me. Your reactions." I sounded like a fucking caveman, but it was all I was capable of at the moment. "You give them freely enough to your viewers. I demand nothing less."

She quirked an eyebrow, putting her hands on her hips in agitation. At least, I thought that was what she was trying to convey. Her rapid breathing told me a different story. "Oh, really? You gonna tip me?"

"Nope. You're gonna give me your true feelings and reactions because you have to. Because I affect you just as much as you affect me."

"You don't know that. I've fucked more men than I can count. The sensations die after a while. The new wears off."

I shook my head. "I don't believe that. Not the way you came apart for me in the truck. Not the way you devoured my cock. A woman doesn't do that shit unless she means it. You might suck me off, but not with the passion you showed. You loved what you did."

"Yeah. I did. Coulda been any cock," she snapped. "Just happened to be yours."

I looked at her for a long time, trying my best to judge how much of that was true and how much was Eden protecting herself.

"OK," I said. "You love sucking cock. You loved sucking mine." A becoming blush swept up her neck to her face and down her chest. She looked away, and her breathing sped up. "Look at me, Eden." She took a shuddering breath before meeting my gaze. "Would any cock do it for you?" I held her gaze, trying to really measure her response. I wasn't sure what I was expecting to see or even what I wanted to see. "Or was it my cock that made you so eager to swallow me down and take my cum from me?"

"Does it matter? You got the result." She didn't look back at me, but she didn't move to cover herself either.

I grabbed her shoulders and gave her a little shake, bringing her gaze back to mine. "It matters to me, Eden!"

"Why?" she cried. "Why do you even care! You got off! Which was what I intended!"

"Because you're not just another woman to me! You're special. You're... special." I couldn't seem to form the words I needed to. I just wasn't ready to admit she was the woman I wanted for my own. Mainly because my pride wouldn't let me. Not when she was so much younger than me. Not when there was a very real chance I could never keep her satisfied.

Eden gave a little sob and threw her naked body into my arms. The next thing I knew, her lips found mine, and I was lost.

I tightened my arms around her, holding her to me as I took over the kiss. A loud groan escaped from someone, and I was pretty sure it was me. She felt so good in my arms, tasted so good on my tongue. I had that one small taste from before, and I knew it couldn't be the end. I would make Eden mine.

Lifting her in my arms, I carried her to the bed. She wrapped herself around me, digging her heels into my lower back. When I laid her down on the bed, she immediately started pulling at my shirt, tugging it from my pants and tunneling her hands under it to get at my bare skin. She let out a little whimper followed by a low purr of pleasure when she ran her palms over my skin. My muscles rippled beneath her touch, and I had to fight to get my pants off instead of just letting her touch and explore to her heart's content.

I stood, jerking the rest of my clothes off before crawling onto the bed. She reached for me, pulling me to her for a searing kiss. There was nothing more I wanted in that moment than to just sink my cock into her wet heat and lose myself in her tight little body, but the one thing I knew with absolute certainty was that this had to fucking blow her mind or I'd never get another chance.

I let her cling to me and explore my mouth for a while, letting her know what I never could with words that this was all about her. We went at her pace. My cock dragged up and down her sex, riding high on her belly with each thrust of my hips. Her arms were wrapped tightly around my neck and mine were around her body as tightly as I could manage. The feel of her skin on mine was the biggest turn-on I'd ever had. Make no mistake, I hadn't been a virgin in a fucking long time. Hell, I'd been married! Had a kid! But this… I was ashamed to admit it, but I wanted Eden more than I'd ever wanted another woman in my life. I had no idea why. Maybe it had just been too long since I'd had sex. Or maybe it was the way I'd stalked Eden's online persona, buying into her sexy presence. Whatever it was, I was ravenous for her.

Knowing I'd never be able to resist simply stuffing my cock inside her and fucking her until I found oblivion if I kept this up much longer, I pulled away from her kisses. The little sounds she was making were driving me crazy! I trailed my lips down her body, kissing, nipping, licking…

"So fuckin' sweet," I murmured against her damp skin. She was actually trembling in my arms, her body lightly coated in sweat. She had the responses of a novice when I knew she was anything but. "Gonna eat you alive, baby. 'Til we both go up in flames."

"Grady." Her voice was soft, a satin caress. It played over my senses like her fingers danced over my skin. She sounded like she looked: like a woman losing herself in her man. Only I could never be the man she needed. At least, that was what I kept telling myself. Deep down, I knew I'd never let her go. She was mine. I just had to figure out a way to justify keeping her.

Looking up her body, holding her gaze with mine, I licked her sweet pussy from opening to clit. Eden cried out, arching her back and thrusting her hips at me while I swirled around her clit over and over. Inserting two fingers inside her, I pumped gently. She was tight, slick, and oh so very hot. Her essence overflowed and wet my hand and her thighs as I worked her pussy, her excitement evident. The responses I coaxed from her were genuine. There was no artifice about her. Everything about Eden was the real deal. And I got the feeling she loved as hard as she played.

The one thing I knew for sure was that she was a woman out of my league. I'd loved my wife with all my heart, but it was a different feeling altogether. With Elizabeth, I'd known her all my life. She and Charlotte had been my world. I'd protected them both with my life, but my love for Elizabeth had been gentle. Caring. We'd grown up together, so we were more like equals than me being the dominant in the relationship. I hadn't really developed those traits until she'd gotten sick, and I'd had to take complete charge. With Eden, what I felt was raw. Primitive. There was nothing gentle about what I felt for her. I wanted to consume her. To wrap her up in my arms and kill anyone who even thought about harming her. Or taking her from me. Which meant this stalker, whoever he was, was a dead man.

With a hard suck to her clit and a light slap to her bare mound, I crawled back up Eden's body, tucked my cock against her entrance, and slid home. We both cried out in ecstasy.

"Fuck me," I muttered. "So fuckin' tight! Gonna come before I'm ready!"

"Grady! Oh, God! Oh, God!"

I moved in her, trying to take my time but knowing it was a lost cause. Eden wrapped her arms and legs around me and thrust her hips at me with a strangled sob. When I tried to keep some semblance of control, she nipped my shoulder and I was just *gone*!

"Fuck!" I shouted as I pulled away, flipping Eden over onto her belly and shoving my cock back inside her again. I lay on top of her, finding her hands and threading my fingers through hers. I held her arms above her head while I fucked her as hard as I could. "Little witch! You think you can play with me?"

"Not play with you!" she cried. "Need to fuck you!"

"Yeah? Well, I'm fuckin' you, Eden. Gonna fuck you so fuckin' hard!"

"Fuck! Grady! Yes!"

I let go of her hands and wrapped my arms around her middle and fucked her with everything in me. I growled and snarled, hardly recognizing myself. Never in my life had I treated a woman like this. When I felt my balls tighten and my cock begin to swell, I found her clit with my fingers and rubbed, spreading her moisture over the little engorged button. She immediately came in a wet rush, squeezing my cock like she wanted to strangle it. I followed her into the madness, my cock erupting in hot, sticky cum.

The second the sensations started to ebb, I rolled us to our sides. I still thrust inside her, but gently now. With more care. My arms were still tightly wrapped around her, and I wanted to stay that way for the rest of my life. My heart pounded. Sweat coated my body. I could barely catch my breath. And in that moment, I found peace like I hadn't had since long before Elizabeth had passed.

With one last, shuddering breath, I found Eden's shoulder where I'd bitten her earlier and lapped softly, then went limp behind her. Her breathing was as ragged as mine. Her hands clenched my forearms, holding me to her as hard as I held her to me.

"You OK?" I was almost afraid to hear the answer, but I had to ask it. I had been in no way gentle with her.

"Yeah," she said, sleepily. She sounded dazed but content. "I'm perfect."

Somehow, I managed to get the covers over both of us. Then, my cock still inside her, my cum leaking out and coating my balls and her inner thighs, I passed out with the woman of my dreams wrapped tightly in my arms.

Chapter Four

Eden

I awoke to the last rays of sunshine peeking through the back window. The curtains had been pulled closed, but the light found a crack and shone directly on my face. It wasn't unpleasant, but it made me realize I was in the bed alone. Grady was nowhere to be found. His scent lingered on my pillow, but the spot next to me was cool.

With a sigh, I sat up and stretched. I was sore, but pleasantly so. It all reminded me of the incredible time I'd had with Grady during our time together throughout the day. He'd woken me twice, and I'd woken him three times. The third time I'd woken him, he'd chuckled, reaching for me eagerly. "You're such a delightful thing," he'd said. Then rocked my world even more than he already had. All in all, it was one of the best days of my life.

On the nightstand, there was a note from Grady telling me he'd gone for supplies. He'd be back with dinner as quickly as he could. I smiled as I read the note. I wasn't a sexual innocent. I hadn't had as many partners as Grady believed -- I'd only had four before him, one of them being Iron. I hadn't had sex with anyone outside of Salvation's Bane since my very first time, and never with someone I cared about. Grady made me rethink the way I viewed sex.

Before, sex had been fun. A pleasant way to pass the time. I loved the attention I got from camming, but it had never fulfilled any emotional needs for me. Iron was a wonderful man, and I got some of what I needed from him, but we didn't love each other. He was good to me, made sure I was taken care of almost as much as my brother did. But he didn't give me what I needed emotionally, and I'm sure I didn't for him either.

Grady, however...

He blew my mind. In all ways. He was an amazing lover, but he was also careful with me. No matter what we did together, he always made sure I was not only satisfied, but he held me afterward. Tightly. He smelled my hair, petted me, murmuring how beautiful and wonderful I was until I went to sleep. Was I in love? No. But I could see myself being with Grady for a while. Abrasive personality aside, I genuinely liked the guy. He was protective, as evidenced by this trip north to Kentucky. He loved his daughter and was willing to give Samson a chance to make her happy because it was what Charlotte wanted. Plus, he wasn't afraid to get his hands dirty to serve justice to people who needed it.

With a smile on my face, I ran through the shower quickly and dressed in my shorts and his shirt from the night before, wanting to be ready when Grady came back so we could talk about our night and how we were going to move forward.

The door opened just as I finished brushing my teeth, and Grady entered. He had some sacks with him, including food and clothing for me. He pulled his sandwich and one of the sodas out of the bag and headed for the door, never having said a word to me or acknowledged me in any way. I thought maybe he was going to lock the door, but he opened it and stepped through.

"Wait!" I hurried over to him, wanting to throw my arms around him, but his hands were full. By design? "Where are you going?"

"I'm eating out here. I need to get a feel for the area before we leave."

"Oh. OK." I had no idea what else to say. He

obviously didn't want to stay with me for whatever reason. Though it hurt, I wasn't about to beg or throw myself at him. "Let me know when you're ready to go."

Without another word or glance at me, Grady left the room. All the warm, fuzzy feelings I'd had vanished on the breeze from the door as it closed. I felt like he'd punched me in the gut. And I had no one to blame but myself. This day should never have happened. We should never have had sex. Somewhere deep inside me, I knew it had been a bad idea, but I'd wanted it so much. Likely, I'd confirmed everything about me Grady despised.

It's behavior like this that caused you problems in the first Goddamned place.

It took every ounce of pride and control I possessed not to break down into tears. But I promised myself right then, I'd try to get through to him. I wasn't going to throw myself at him or try to engage him in sex again. Even though he'd been the one to engage me the night before, he didn't want me. It wasn't the way I wished he felt, but there was nothing I could do about his feelings about the way I'd lived my life. I'd embraced my sexuality. Grady couldn't get past that. And it was OK. He was from a different generation. His daughter was only a couple of years younger than me. I just wished it didn't hurt so damned much.

Clearing my throat to try to rid myself of the fucking lump growing there, I looked at the sack he'd tossed on the bed. Not only were there a couple of pairs of jeans and four T-shirts, but socks, underwear, toiletries, and a pair of shoes. He might have regretted our day in bed, but he was still taking care of me. Which kind of made me want to cry even more.

I glanced at my phone. I wanted like anything to call Charlotte. In the short time she'd been in my life, Lottie had become my best friend. Someone I loved and counted on when I'd only ever relied on my brother, and only when it had been strictly necessary. If anyone knew what made her dad tick, it would be her.

Decision made, I punched Lottie's contact and waited for her to pick up.

"You gettin' freaky with my dad, Eden?"

I couldn't help but laugh. Leave it to Lottie to make me feel better. "If I am, do you really want to know?"

"Not at all." She laughed. "Just felt like it was the expected question."

After our giggling died down, I felt like crying. Just having Lottie there and talking to me broke down my defenses and made me want to tell her everything.

"Remember when you told me to text you if things got out of hand?" I sniffed, trying to keep from breaking down crying.

"Yeah? You said they already were out of hand." I could hear the humor in Lottie's voice, but also a hint of weariness. Like she could sense something was off.

"Well, they're out of hand."

There was a silence while she thought about this. "But I take it not in a good way?"

"I'm not sure." I sniffed again. This time, a little sob escaped.

"Eden, are you OK?" Now Lottie was dead serious.

"Not really." I told her everything that had happened. "I don't know what to do. I can't make him accept my past, but I'm not sure I can leave him alone either. I'm cringing even talking to you about this because he's your dad, but he kind of rocked my world."

"Yeah. Don't want the dirty details, but I swear to you, Dad is a good guy. I don't know why he said all that stuff about your behavior and shit, but he's not like that, Eden."

"I figured it was just our age difference. Which brings up another question. I didn't plan this, Lottie. I wasn't the one who started it, well other than texting him the naughty pictures. That was just to distract him while you and Samson worked out your shit. But how do you feel about it? I don't want you uncomfortable or angry."

"Stop right there, Eden." Charlotte's whole tone changed. She was very serious now. "My mother passed away ten years ago. She was the love of my dad's life. After we buried her, he changed, and not for the better. He threw himself into his job, and there have been many times I've been afraid he wouldn't be careful..." She trailed off, and I heard her own sniffle. "I'm afraid he'll get hurt because he doesn't care about life anymore." She took a shuddering breath. "Since he met you, he's changed again. There's still an edge to him, but I've seen him focusing on you more and more. Even before he found out about the stalker thing. He might be fighting it, but he's taken an interest in you."

"Shoulda known you'd talked to him. Does he say anything about me?" God, could I sound any more pathetic?

"Nope. But he doesn't have to. I can hear it in his voice, Eden. You've affected him. My advice? Push him. Make him talk about what happened today."

Yeah. That wasn't happening. "Have you met your dad? Pretty sure no one pushes him on anything."

She laughed. "Which is why it will work. And only with you. Trust me on this."

I wasn't sure I could do that. At least, not right away. And not without some alcohol or being really, *really* mad. Though I had no doubt Grady would protect me if I needed it, I also knew he'd put me in my place faster than I could say fuck.

"I'll see what I can manage. There's only so much courage in my body, Lottie."

"I have faith in you. You should have a little faith in my judgment of my father." Thank goodness she sounded like she was laughing at me. If I'd managed to hurt Charlotte's feelings because I was feeling the sting, I'd never forgive myself.

"I do have faith in you, sister. You take care of my big brother."

"Oh, believe me. I'm definitely taking very good care of him."

"Don't wanna know… *Do not* want to know." We laughed as we hung up.

It wasn't long after that the door opened, and Grady looked at me. "You ready? We need to get moving. I want to make it to Kentucky before daybreak." He looked irritated. "Shoulda just pushed through this morning but I didn't want to take a chance on being followed."

"Ouch," I muttered.

His eyes narrowed. "What?"

"Nothing. All packed and ready to go." Packed meant everything in the room that was ours was in a fucking Walmart bag. 'Cause, you know, no suitcase, backpack, or purse.

He gave me a hard stare. "Good. Get moving." He turned to leave, and I gave him a snappy salute behind his back as he hurried out the door.

"Asshole."

"Heard that," he called from outside but said nothing else.

The ride to the Bones MC clubhouse was *extremely* uneventful. And boring. Every time I turned the radio on, he turned it off. When I tried to engage in small talk, he ignored me.

"Are you going to give me the silent treatment forever?"

"Nope. Just until we get to Bones, then you can find someone else to keep you entertained."

"What's your fucking problem, *Lawdawg*?"

"Don't call me that," he snapped.

"Why? Not sophisticated enough for a small-town sheriff? What should I call you? Mr. Bassett?" I pitched my voice higher like I was a little girl. "Hey, Mr. Bassett? Can Lottie come out and play?"

A muscle ticked in his jaw, and his forearms bunched where he gripped the steering wheel tight. At two and ten. He said nothing.

"So, I want to know what your problem with me is, Grady. We got along fine today. What changed while I slept?"

He winced slightly. "Today never should have happened, Eden. It won't happen again."

"Why would you say that? I thought you had a good time. *I* had a great time."

"I'm too old for you. I also have more responsibilities than keeping a girl like you out of trouble."

I could feel the color rising in my face, my anger spiking. "A girl like me?" I bit the question through clenched teeth.

"Yes. You're always going to be in some kind of trouble, and I have a whole town of people depending on me."

"You know what? Stop the fucking truck. I'll fuckin' *walk* to Kentucky before I take you one more fucking mile away from your precious little town!"

"Shut up, Eden. I'm taking you to Kentucky, then I'm leaving. Cain can keep you safe until we track down this son of a bitch."

"Wait. You brought me all this way just to *dump me off*?"

* * *

Grady

"What did you expect?" I was in way over my head with this girl. She would have me running in circles if I let her, and the shit of it was, I wanted to let her. The day we'd spent in bed had awakened something inside me I never knew was there. The more I thought about it, the more I realized it was more than simple protectiveness and possessiveness. I felt like a caveman. Just like I'd probably looked when I'd carried her out of the Black Reign clubhouse over my shoulder. That was who I was when I was with her. Hell, it was who I was when I *wasn't* with her.

I hadn't actually left the little bed and breakfast when I'd stepped outside to get away from her. I'd paid one of the girls running the place that morning to go shopping for her and to bring back something to eat. No way I would have left Eden alone for something so frivolous. And trust one of those app companies? No way. Besides, it would give us a digital footprint for a tech savvy bastard to follow us. I never turned on the GPS on my phone, and Shotgun, the tech guy at Black Reign, assured me her GPS was permanently disabled.

But, to answer her question, no. I originally had

no intention of dumping her off. I just wasn't sure I trusted myself with her now.

"What exactly did you expect, Eden? I'm not the white knight rescuing damsels in distress. I'm a fuckin' law enforcement officer. My job is to catch criminals. This guy stalking you might not have done anything criminal against you yet, but my gut says that's where he's headed. So, I'm gonna do what I'm best at and catch the bastard." And kill him. But I didn't say that to her.

"What about serve and protect?" she fired off. "What if I need you to protect me?"

"That's why I'm bringin' you to someplace off the main drag and putting you with people I trust. Cain and I served together in the Corp. He's the most trustworthy, dangerous person I know. He and his club will protect you. I'll eliminate the threat to you. It's what I do."

"Then tell me, O protector, what the fuck was all this today about? I get the feeling you don't go around screwing every woman you come across. If you do, then why are you giving me shit over my lifestyle choices, huh? And for the record," she stabbed her finger in my direction, driving home whatever point she was about to make, "I've had exactly five lovers, Grady. Five! I'm not some kind of sexual deviant who sleeps with every Tom, Dick, and Harry who crosses my path."

That shocked me. Then I thought about the videos I'd watched. Most of them with men in them -- especially the latter ones -- paired her with Iron. I'd noticed a couple others from earlier in the series they had posted, but no more than two or three. I wasn't really good at judging men's dicks, but I was really good at recognizing tattoos.

I narrowed my eyes, and my nostrils flared. "All of them from Black Reign?"

"All but two."

"Callin' bullshit on that one, baby. I know there was at least three different guys you fucked on camera. Was one of your men from outside the club?"

"No, Grady. My first lover wasn't from Black Reign, and I learned my lesson. You were the second guy I've been with outside Black Reign. Guess I didn't learn the first lesson well enough, eh?"

Fuck me raw. I wanted to throttle the little wench. "You sayin' I'm not good enough for you because I don't belong to your brother's club?"

"Not at all. I'm saying you're not good enough for me because you're a fucking asshole! Fuck you, Grady Bassett! And go to fucking hell!"

OK, so, maybe the "girl like you" comment was a poor choice of words. I wasn't intentionally trying to run her off, but maybe it'd work out that way. "You're too young for me, Eden. And I'm way to fuckin' old for you. Accept it. Get over it."

"You fuckin' get over it," she muttered.

The rest of the trip was spent in silence. It was what I'd wanted, but not like this.

I'd reflected on everything that had happened over the day. I wasn't a fantastic lover. I didn't have women flocking to me in droves to experience my sexual prowess. I'd had a few hookups since Elizebeth had passed, but usually one-night stands that weren't nearly as satisfying as I'd wanted them to be. In the end, I'd mostly just jacked off and been done with it. I didn't want a replacement for Elizabeth, and I would never risk hurting Charlotte by bringing a woman to her mother's home.

And, fuck it all, Eden was young enough to be

my daughter! It was the whole reason I'd objected to Samson taking up with Charlotte. How could I justify being with Eden when I still didn't fully approve of my daughter's choice?

Fuck.

When we rolled through the Bones compound gates, I wanted to sink down to my knees and thank God the trip was finally over. I could grab a quick bite and head back to Florida tonight. I'd have to stop in a few hours, but at least I could put some distance between me and Eden.

Because, God help me, I was already in love with her. Her spirit was just bright and beautiful and everything I wasn't. She was fresh and free as a summer breeze, but that was the whole problem. There was no way she didn't get tired of my brooding and controlling ways. She'd leave me, and then I'd have lost two women I loved. Only, losing Eden would devastate me on a whole other level. I'd lost a life partner in Elizabeth, and while I'd loved my wife with my whole heart, if I lost Eden, I'd have lost the love of my life. I knew it like I knew my own name. Eden was it for me. For the rest of my life. It would devastate me beyond anything I could recover from to have her in my life, then lose her because of the man I was. Best to leave now before she entrenched herself even more deeply into my heart.

The second I slammed the trunk into park I took out my phone and stabbed Cain's name on my contact list. I slid from the vehicle and shut the door harder than strictly necessary, not waiting to see if Eden followed.

"Yeah. We're here. Might be trouble following us, but I don't think so."

"I've got you a room all set up. The two of you

can stay here as long as you need." Cain was straightforward, to the point as always.

"Not stayin'. She is."

There was a pause. "You're not staying with her? El Diablo indicated you'd insist on seeing to her protection."

Motherfucker. I was having a fuckin' chat with that fucker when I got back. "He thought wrong," I growled. It wasn't a tone of voice I took with Cain often. Or ever, really.

"Watch the tone," Cain snapped back. "Don't know what's put the bee in your saddle, but this is my territory. Not yours, Grady."

I took a breath. "Been a long trip."

"Then take some time and rest. Find you a girl and get some relief if you're not with Samson's sister. But remember we're helping you out here. Not the other way around."

"Noted, brother." I added the "brother" to soften the sting so I didn't actually have to apologize to Cain, and he knew it as well as I did. "Tell me you at least got us separate rooms. Not sure I can take another night -- or day -- in the same room with her."

"She that hard on the eyes?"

"No."

When I said nothing else, Cain chuckled. "Well, I'm sorry to tell you, space is limited. I had one room. You two get to share it. Unless, that is, you find another woman to hook up with while you're here. Club girls want to share their beds -- you're welcome to take your pick."

"I'm sure sharing a club girl's bed would be loads of fun." I'd meant it sarcastically, but it just came out tired.

I turned around and saw Eden not three steps

behind me. Her mouth was open in a gasp, a shocked and hurt expression on her face before she shut it down. She only missed a couple of steps before putting her head down and marching past me into the clubhouse, her bag of belongings clutched to her chest like a kid going to stay at a distant cousin's house she hated.

"Fuck," I sighed.

"Something wrong?"

I'd totally forgotten Cain was still there. "Yeah. Nothing I can't fix with a shovel to dig my own grave."

The bastard chuckled. "I see. Girl heard you, did she?"

"Fucker," I said before ending the call. The very last thing in the world I wanted to do was hurt Eden like this. I was a bastard for wanting to leave her, but there was no way I wanted her to think I was replacing her in my bed. Not like this. I knew the truth that I'd never have another woman as long as I lived. Since I couldn't tell her that, I just wanted to make a clean break. If I was gonna do it, it had to be here. But not like this.

Stepping into the clubhouse, I scanned the common room for Eden, but couldn't find her. If she was with one of Cain's bikers, I'd fuckin' kill the bastard. I was just about to start tearing the place apart when my phone rang. A quick look told me Samson was wanting an update on our travels. I winced, not wanting to take the fucking call.

I debated for all of three seconds before I shoved the phone back in my pocket. Fuck him. But the call came again. Then again. And yet again. When he called back the fifth time, I sighed and picked it up.

"Told you I'd call once we were at the compound and settled. What the fuck do you want?"

"We agreed you'd wait for me to get backup ready to come with you. What the fuck, Bassett?" Yeah. Samson was pissed.

"Had a change of plan. Besides, we're here. No tail. Nothing happened." I winced. Something had *definitely* happened.

"I've got Shadow, Archangel, and El Segador headed your way. The only reason you get to live is because you took my sister straight to a club El Diablo respects and approves of."

"I don't have to justify myself to you, Samson. I did the right thing in the best way possible. Having a posse of motorcycles surrounding us would have led the fuck straight to the front fuckin' door!"

"You know we don't work that way. You're deflecting. What the fuck happened, Bassett!"

"Nothing happened! We made it here safe and sound. I'd let you talk to the little wench, but she fuckin' disappeared the second she ran into the fucking clubhouse."

"Disappeared? What the fuck?"

"What can I say, Samson? My charming personality is lost on the girl."

There was a long silence before Samson asked me the one question I did not want to answer. And he asked it in a tone of voice that made me realize he'd already figured out the answer.

"Did you sleep with my sister, Bassett?"

In my life, I'd learned to do some despicable things. I could kill as easily as breathing if it was warranted. I'd disappear the body and no one would ever be the wiser. I could torture a man six ways to Sunday and not lose a moment's sleep. What I could never do was lie worth a good Goddamn.

"We stopped at a bed and breakfast on the way

here. One room. Of course, I slept with her. You wanted me outside in the vehicle where I couldn't protect her?"

"You ain't no kind of Marine if you can't go a day without sleep, you fucker. Why'd you stop in the first Goddamned place?"

"To avoid traveling during the fuckin' day where any fuckin' body and his Goddamned brother could fuckin' see us."

Another silence before Samson spoke again. "I'm thinkin' that ain't no answer, Bassett. So Imma ask you one more fuckin' time. This time I'll put it bluntly. Did you fuck my sister?"

No way to deflect that. "Yeah, Samson. I fucked her."

I expected a string of very foul, very inventive curses but was met with only silence. I thought he might have hung up, but a quick look at the phone screen told me the line was still active.

"If you fucked her, and she ran off the first chance she got, it obviously wasn't a pleasant experience." Strangely, the man sounded kind of under control. More so than I was when I suspected he was having sex with my daughter. "So what the fuck happened." It wasn't a question. More like a demand.

"That's not your business," I said, knowing Samson would never take that answer.

"Not good enough," he snapped.

I dug my thumb and finger into my eyes, then scrubbed my head with the same hand. "I'm not the man for her, Samson. It was a mistake, me taking her. She deserves a better man than me. And I…"

"You pushed her away," Samson finished for me. "In other words, you hurt her."

"I'm sure I did."

"Intentionally."

I winced. "Well, when you say it like that, it sounds worse than it actually was."

"Let me fill in some blanks. Feel free to stop me if I'm wrong." Samson sounded as pissed as I'd ever heard a man. I had no doubt that, if he were in front of me, we'd be in the middle of a brawl that would make the one we'd had at Tito's Diner over my daughter look like a Sunday outing. "You took her to task over her lifestyle. Choosing to attack her for her being a cam girl in the club instead of a pristine little angel like you'd prefer her to be. Instead of just telling her she deserves better than you, like you told me, you made her feel like she was the one lacking."

"And she might have overheard part of a conversation between me and Cain and took it out of context," I muttered.

"Gonna need that explanation too, Bassett."

"Fuck." I swore softly after giving Samson the rundown. I had no idea why I'd just confessed how badly I'd hurt Eden, especially to Samson. I didn't even like the bastard. Maybe I was trying to punish myself. Asking for the beating I knew I deserved.

"Another change of plan, Bassett. I'm headed that way now. You got until I get there to make this right with Eden in whatever way you choose. But if she's not good, the mountains of Southeastern Kentucky can hide a body just as easily as the fuckin' swamps of Florida. I will cut you up into little pieces and feed you to the fuckin' pigs." The line went dead.

I wasn't worried about Samson. Or even the brothers he had on the way up here. I was worried about Eden, because Samson was right. It was a chickenshit thing to say to her. The whole thing about me sharing a club girl's bed wasn't my fault, but she'd likely have stayed and made me explain if I hadn't already made a mess of things.

Yeah. Not my finest moment. I was fucking up every single way I could with this girl, and I didn't seem to be able to stop.

Chapter Five

Eden

When I stormed into the clubhouse of this new MC, I had no idea what I was doing. I knew better. I was a guest. Learning the rules and being respectful was the only way to do this, and I'd just breached a major round of protocol. When I was approached by a big guy with a petite woman at his side, I figured I was getting ready to be called out. Instead the woman had a welcoming smile on her face. True to biker form, the other guy just eyed me up and down, sizing me up.

"Hey there," the woman said. "I'm Angel and this is Cain. He's president of Bones. You must be Eden."

I took the hand she offered, struggling to meet her gaze for fear I'd burst into tears. This wasn't any of their business, and the last thing I needed was to bring emotional baggage to another club.

"Yeah. I'm Eden. My brother, Samson, is the VP of Black Reign in Lake Worth."

"El Diablo said you might be in some trouble with a stalker," Cain said gently. "Just so you know, you'll be protected here as if you were our own."

I glanced up at him. "You sayin' that because you know Grady's gonna run back to Kentucky the second he can?" Cain said nothing, just looked at me steadily. Angel gasped and looked up at Cain in alarm.

"I thought you said Grady Bassett was her protector? As in, he was staying with her as her man."

Cain seemed to choose his words carefully, never taking his eyes off me. I ducked my head and looked away. "I was led to believe that, yes."

I heard footsteps behind me and glanced back, wincing when I saw Grady coming up behind me.

Fuck.

"We'll need a room," Grady said. "Both of us."

"Done told you the situation, Grady," Cain said evenly.

"I'll make a separate room," Angel said hastily. She took my hand and urged me deeper into the compound. "I'll put you next to me and Cain."

"Thought you said there was only one room left," Grady said accusingly. I wasn't sure who he was talking to, but the situation was clear.

"You asked for separate rooms," I whispered, looking back over my shoulder at Grady as Angel pulled me along. He met my gaze but said nothing. I did my best to harden my gaze before turning away and letting Angel lead me away.

"I take it there was something between the two of you?"

"No," I said, hoping like hell the woman would take the hint and let it be.

"Please don't think I'm trying to pry, but I need to know what to expect. The club girls here aren't as aggressive as they are in other clubs, but they can still make your life difficult."

"If he wants one, I'm not gonna lose sleep over it."

Angel sighed. "I see. Well, if you need us, you can always find one of the club ol' ladies on this floor. No one is up here other than us and our men. I put you here to make sure you're protected. Cain insisted even before we knew Grady might not stay."

"It's fine. Really." I managed a small smile as she opened the door and handed me a key.

"It locks, but you don't really need the key. The only time anyone locks their door is if they don't want to be disturbed."

I nodded. "Same with Reign." It was a way to fill the silence when I really just wanted to go inside and lick my wounds. "Look. Thanks for this. I appreciate it. I'm sorry if I'm not good company just now. Once I've had some real sleep, I'll be better. I swear."

"Hey. No sweat." Angel waved my apology away. "Men are difficult in the best of situations. It seems like this might not be the best of situations for you right now."

"Guess not," I agreed.

"Get some rest. If you want to come down later, there's usually a party going on."

"Will you be there?"

"Me? No." Angel laughed a little. "Parties aren't my thing. But most of the rest of the women will be there with their men. If you'd like, I could take you down and introduce you, so you'll be a little more comfortable."

"Oh, no. If I decide to go, I'll be fine. It's an MC." I smiled. "I know how to behave at an MC party."

"OK. If you need me, I'm right across the hall." She indicated the door.

I shut the door and sagged against it. Maybe when I left, Grady would have just left. Like he said. That would probably be the best situation I could hope for.

My time at Bones had every possibility of being the very thing to turn my life around. I was a cam girl at Reign because I wanted to be independent. It was also the only way to get laid when everyone knew my big brother was the Vice President. I mean, Iron was a steady lay, but only because we just got on together well. He was a good fuck buddy, but that's as far as it went. No one else in the club would touch me, and the cam crew stopped once Iron and I hooked up. Just out of respect for him.

I didn't really want another man but having someone to cleanse my palate of Grady might be nice. A rough-and-tumble guy who could show me a good time, then get the fuck out so I could... have a fucking breakdown in private.

Who the fuck was I kidding? There was never going to be another man for me other than Grady Bassett.

I gave it a couple of days, holing up in my room by myself. I came down to get meals and brought them all back to my room so I could mope in peace. I talked with Charlotte a few times, and her answer was always the same. Take it to him. Confront him. Make him tell me he doesn't want me. According to her, Grady was the worst liar. He hated it when people lied to him, so he never bothered to learn to lie himself. Still, I wasn't sure. The only positive was, the few times I'd had guys from Bones hit on me, Grady had had a talk with the guy, and he never approached me again. If you could call that a positive. It would have been if Grady had then followed through and come to me. But he hadn't.

Fucker.

As I was sitting in the window seat, reading, trying to reset my mind and ground myself, there was a knock at my door. For some stupid reason, I thought it would be Grady at the door and had to fight myself to keep from rushing to throw the door open.

Outside was a striking woman with red hair and bright blue eyes. She had a warm smile on her face. "I'm Darcy. We haven't met, but Angel thought you might need a friend."

"I appreciate it, but I'm good." I smiled, trying to take the sting out. When Darcy's smile faltered, I realized I'd failed miserably.

"O-OK." Darcy took a breath. "I just thought you might want to join the other ol' ladies and me at the Boneyard. There's a local band playing, and they're pretty good. It might take your mind off things?"

"You know, you're right," I said, taking a deep breath to stave off the disappointment. "I could be here awhile. Might as well have a good time while I'm here."

"That's the spirit!" Darcy's winning smile was back. "Come on. I think Bohannon's driving us tonight. The others will likely show up, but they at least try to give us the illusion it's a true girls night out."

"So they always go with you on girls' night out?" Were the men going because of her and her stalker?

"Yep. Always. Something about making sure other men don't hit on us, but honestly. We're with bikers. I don't see the danger."

I thought about snagging my cell but thought better of it. No one would be calling, and I could give a flying fuck if I missed a call from Grady. Feeling a little better, I headed downstairs with Darcy to find several other women waiting in the common room.

"Oh, good! You talked her into it!" A short, curvy woman with dark curls and brilliant blue eyes reached out a hand. "I'm Rose. Torpedo's woman."

"Torpedo is the VP of Bones?" I'd heard the name.

"You've met my husband, then?"

I shook my head. "No, but I've heard Samson talk about him. My brother respects him."

"We're going to have such a good time! Come on." Rose's smile was beautiful. The other woman was probably in her mid-thirties like the others. I felt like the odd woman out being ten or fifteen years younger than them, but not because the other women were less than generous. Quite the opposite. They talked my ears off the whole way to the club. By the time we got there, I was laughing so much my belly hurt and smiling so much my face hurt.

Besides Rose -- whose name was actually Ambrosia -- and Darcy, there were two other women with us. Rain and Magenta. I'd forgotten who their men were, but they were all members of Bones. When we got to the club, they headed for a table in the corner as if it were theirs by default. When we got there, three men were sitting at the table, but hastily beat a retreat when Ambrosia raised an eyebrow.

"It's Friday night, boys," she said as they scattered without so much as a mutter, but with a few excuse me's and, "Sorry, Rose. We forgot what night it was."

"Wow," I laughed. "Your reputation precedes you?"

Rose shrugged. "Might have had a run in with some big, badass bikers when they wouldn't let us have our table in the past."

"I'm sure the fact that Arkham and Sword were glaring daggers at them from two tables over had nothing to do with it," Rain said with a sigh before we all burst into giggles.

When the server approached us, she had drinks already made for my companions.

"What'll you have, honey?" she asked me as she set the glasses down.

"Um, maybe a Bud Light?"

"Anything you want, sweety. Draft or bottle?"

"Draft," I said with a smile. The music was starting up, and I was getting excited to just have a normal night out with the girls. They might not be my friends, but I had the feeling they could be if I were here long enough. Maybe I'd take a break from Black Reign and Florida for a while. If things went smoothly, after Samson got my stalker taken care of, maybe I'd ask Angel if she could get permission for me to stay with Bones.

"Hey, sweety." The big, burly man was addressing me. He had several scars running over a face that had once been handsome. Even now, as I looked at him, I could see he would be scary in the right circumstances, but I'd been around my share of scarred, tattooed men. This guy had an easy grin and mischief in his eyes I couldn't ignore. "Wanna dance?"

I returned his smile and took his hand. "Absolutely."

"Name's Carnage," he said by way of introduction. "I hear you're that lil' bit from Black Reign. Eden, is it?"

"Yeah. How do you know my name?"

"Honey, the club girls knew everything there was to know about you the second you walked in the clubhouse."

That made my smile falter. "Look, I don't --"

"Relax, honey. Ain't no one here judgin' or expectin' anything from you." He was suddenly serious as he pulled me to my feet. "Just dancin' with a beautiful woman. That's all I want."

It was enough to ruin my good mood, but I tried to shake it off. If everyone at Bones knew I was a cam girl, how long before I was hit on by every horny biker in the vicinity? At Reign, they knew not to give me shit because Samson would kick their asses. But what about Bones?

"Maybe this isn't a good idea," I said, pulling my hand away.

"Hey," Carnage said, raising his hands in a nonthreatening gesture. "I only want to dance. Maybe buy you another drink. Ain't gonna make a move on ya." He grinned at me. "Now, you decide you want to make a move on me? Yeah. I might take you up on it. I know my pretty face is hard to resist."

I rolled my eyes. "Does that line even work?"

"Sure," he shrugged. "All the time. Workin' on you?"

"Not in the least," I said, finding myself grinning despite my disquiet. "Fine. One dance," I said. "But only because I feel sorry for you. Your personality is so standoffish you'll likely never get a girl to dance with you."

"Now, that's the spirit." He grinned, then pulled me to the dance floor.

* * *

Grady

Going to the Boneyard was supposed to have been a way to relax. Instead, I was finding it an exercise in frustration. When the big, scarred man named Carnage by his brothers swept Eden into his arms out on the dance floor, I wanted to pull my sidearm and shoot the motherfucker. She was way too young for him. And if I couldn't have her because of her age, then no other son of a bitch would either.

I watched them for three dances. When Carnage bent his head like he was going to kiss Eden, I lost my shit.

I crossed the distance between me and the happy couple. Eden had her back to me, but Carnage saw me coming and swung Eden around to put himself between me and her. I grudgingly gave him brownie points for that. Didn't mean I wasn't throwin' the son of a bitch a beating. I grabbed his shoulder and spun him around.

"Get the fuck out, Carnage." Just looking at the guy made me want to punch him in the face. He was way too Goddamned old for Eden.

"Just dancin' with the lady. Danced three songs with her, and she didn't object once."

"She's objectin' now."

Carnage looked over his shoulder at Eden. "You want me to leave?"

"I never said that," Eden said. She looked everywhere but at me.

"She ain't gotta say it. I'm sayin' it for her."

The big man didn't back down an inch. "You don't get to say it for her. You ain't her man." Carnage smirked.

It was all I could do to not shoot the guy on the spot. "She tell you that? Because you're dead fuckin' wrong. She's my woman, and you're fuckin' tresspassin'."

Carnage lashed out, throwing a punch I easily deflected. He threw another one. I blocked. I got the feeling it was half-hearted, but he still swung at me.

"What the fuck?" Eden screeched behind us. "Grady, what the fuck are you doing?"

"He's the one takin' swings at me. Not the other way around, Eden."

Finally, one of Carnage's punches connected. The men in the bar let up a cheer.

"I didn't start this fight, but I'm damn sure gonna end it." I went low, taking Carnage in the midsection, following it up with a backhanded swing Carnage managed to block.

"Lady's with me until she says she ain't." Carnage tightened his fists, making the muscles and veins in his arms stand out. A show of intimidation.

He lunged for me again. This time, I unleashed hell on the man. Carnage and I fought. Blood flying, grunting. Destruction of property in the bar was involved. The next thing I knew my ass was being hauled off the big man where I straddled his chest and pounded on his face. Carnage still fought, but someone had had enough.

A single shot was fired, and everyone stopped. I looked up to see the old man they called Pops at the bar with a smoking shotgun in his hands. Reminded me of an Old West movie. I had the inane thought to wonder if he'd just blasted a hole in the roof of the bar and if he'd expect me to fix it when Cain strolled up to me and Carnage.

"Not sure what the fuck went down, but you do not fight in my fuckin' bar."

I nodded to Eden. "She's my woman."

Cain raised an eyebrow. "Well, she was dancin' with Carnage. Seems to me like you ain't locked that down yet."

Eden shoved her way between all the badass bikers to stand beside me. Then she bent and picked up a chair leg. Or was it a table leg? Anyway, teeth bared with a savage growl, she swung at me with all her might. I raised my arm to block her and nearly got my arm broke for the effort. The pain was instant and fierce.

"Bastard!" she screeched. "You don't want me, but you don't want anyone else to have me?"

"Eden, just settle down."

"Set..." She blinked. "*Settle*? Are you out of your fucking mind?"

"We'll talk about this when we get back to the clubhouse." That sounded reasonable. I was winded from the fight, but knew it was imperative I projected strength with her. No way Eden responded to a man who was less than her equal.

"Go fuck yourself, Grady!" She swung again, and I caught the chair leg, snagging it from her grip and tossing it aside.

"We can go quietly or I can carry you out, Eden. Take your pick."

"You can carry yourself out and get the fuck on back to Lake Worth! I'm staying in Kentucky at this club. Making a new life for myself, and it doesn't include you!"

I hated public confrontation. I hated airing my dirty laundry in front of anyone, especially a group of strangers. Most of all, I hated that Eden was bucking my claim on her when I hadn't meant to claim her in the first Goddamned place.

"Now, Eden," I growled at her. "Come with me. We'll talk about this."

I glanced at Carnage to make sure the man was leaving well enough alone. The bastard had gotten to his feet and was moving toward me with purpose.

"Fuck," I bit out. "I'm too fuckin' old for this shit."

"She's not going anywhere." Carnage moved next to me, meeting my gaze with a steady one of his own. I respected that he was protecting Eden, but honestly, she didn't need protecting from me. "She stays with me. I know for a fact you're not her daddy," Carnage said. "Her daddy's dead, and Samson at Black Reign is her brother and under his protection." He looked me up and down like I was somehow less than he was. "You're just some small-town lawdawg who thinks his shit don't stink."

"Doesn't change the fact she's not stayin' with you."

"She will if she wants to. Eden?" Carnage didn't take his eyes off me.

"I don't want trouble on account of me," she said, more subdued than she had been.

Pops piped up. "Well, lil' bit. Looks like you got it. You need to make a decision. If it helps, I'll vouch for Carnage. He's a good man, but he's a club man. Club will always come first with him."

I gave Pops an impatient look. "She's coming with me. End of discussion." I snagged Eden's hand to drag her out of the bar. Carnage moved to put himself between me and Eden and the door, not backing down an inch.

"Make your choice, Eden," he said. "I'll protect you if he's stalking you."

Eden sighed. "He's not stalking me. He's trying to keep the stalker away from me. I'll go with him. For now."

"You need me, you text. Got it?"

"You got his fuckin' phone number?" I asked, turning to glare at Eden.

"I do. It's what people who want to see each other again do," Eden snapped. "Now, get me the fuck outta here or leave by yourself. I'm tired of playing your fucking games!" That got chuckles around the bar.

Snagging her hand, I let her to my truck, then back to the fucking Bones compound. We might be in a strange place surrounded by strange men, but it was the most secure place in the area. And I had people watching out for me. Cain was one of my oldest friends. I trusted him with my life. More importantly, I trusted him with Eden's.

"What the fuck are you doing?" Eden asked when I didn't take her to her room but proceeded to a different area of the clubhouse.

"Taking you to your room."

"My room is on the other end. Second floor. You know. In the middle of the fuckin' clubhouse. You're in the wrong place."

"Kicked a prospect out of his room. Takin' you to my room."

"What the fuck is wrong with you?" she yelled at me, digging in her heels, refusing to go another step willingly. I just scooped her up and continued down the hall until I stood in front of the room I'd taken over.

I opened the door and shoved her inside, never letting go of her hand. Once the door was shut and locked, I jerked her back into my arms and took her mouth in a kiss.

She fought. At first. But when she opened her mouth, I took advantage, sweeping my tongue inside and deepening my kiss. My arms were tight around her, holding her to me as if she could vanish if I wasn't careful. That feeling of homecoming blanketed me as I continued to kiss and coax her response. This was where I needed to be. The woman I needed to make mine.

With a grunt, I lifted her, urging her legs around my waist. Somehow, I made it to the bed and lowered her to it, following her with my bigger body. I didn't stop kissing her, and she kept her arms around me. I knew I needed to pull back soon, to make sure she was good with what we were doing, but I wanted to assert my claim. Let her know she was mine in no uncertain terms. At least, for now. I'd think about the longer implications once I'd gotten this insanity out of the way.

I pressed her into the mattress, wrapping my arms tightly around her and situating my body between her legs. I knew she could feel my cock rubbing over her mound and flexed my hips once just to emphasize it.

"Grady," she gasped between kisses. "What are you doing?"

"Encouraging you to be very naughty," I answered, my tone gruff. "From now on, you want to do this, you do it with me."

She gave a strangled little chuckle. "You're not making any sense."

"We'll talk after," I bit out. "Right now, I need to fuck you more than I need to fuckin' breathe."

"Oh, God!"

I must have hit her clit in just the right way because Eden arched into me, rocking her hips along my shaft, creating the most delicious friction. "Fuck, Eden! Love the way you fuckin' move!"

I whipped my shirt over my head and urged her to do the same. Eden didn't need much encouragement. Once I urged her in that direction, she rid herself of all her clothes. I still had my jeans on, but it was just as well. I wasn't ready to fuck her yet. No matter how much I wanted to, I absolutely would not be selfish with this woman. She deserved more, and I would fuckin' give it to her if it fuckin' killed me.

Lowering myself on top of her, I held my weight on one straightened arm as I laved her nipple with the flat of my tongue. She cried out and arched to me, wrapping her arms around my neck and holding me to her. Her tits were a good handful, her nipples perfect for sucking. And, fuck, I sucked them. Over and over. One, then the other. Eden squirmed in my arms, whimpering and crying out several times before I abandoned her breasts and trailed kisses, licks, and nips down her torso to her sweet, bare mound.

Her pussy wept with her desire, her clit pulsing under my tongue. Her pussy was so fucking sweet I groaned as I feasted. Eden trembled beneath my touch, whimpering. She sounded as needy as I felt, and I was determined to make this good for her. I knew I could. Had several times already. But this was the first time since I'd admitted to myself she was mine. When I made it clear to her, it would be fresh off the most pleasure she'd ever had in her life.

"Grady! Fuck!"

"Let it go, baby. Give me your orgasm. Come on my tongue. Now!" I knew she responded to dirty talk, even if she didn't do it much herself. Probably because she had to during her cam shows. Which I needed to talk to her about later. If she insisted on doing them, we'd do them as a couple. Because, even with a stalker after her, I knew I'd never deny her something she needed. If it was just a matter of earning her keep for the club, though, fuck that shit. She was with me. She didn't need to earn her Goddamned keep.

Eden shrieked as her orgasm washed over her. Her fingers tunneled through my hair and pulled me where she needed me. She ground her cunt on my face, taking the pleasure I freely offered to her.

"That's it, Eden. You take what you need," I said between licks at her clit. "You will never leave my arms without being completely satisfied. You hear me, girl? Never!"

Eden gasped for breath and sweat erupted over her skin as I crawled up her body. I shoved my pants down my hips as I went, not wanting to actually separate myself from her. Once I lay on top of her, my hips pinning hers, I rocked from side to side, positioning myself just where I wanted to be. My cock was nestled between her lips, slipping through her moisture with ease.

"Grady," she whispered as she pulled me down for a kiss. "Need you."

"I got you, baby," I said, kissing her with all the passion I had in me. "Are you ready?"

"Please! Oh, God, please!"

"Look at me, Eden." I positioned myself at her entrance, stilling my movements even thought I thought I'd fucking die if I didn't sink into her body. "Fuckin' look at me!"

Her eyes snapped to mine, their depths filled with a lustful haze. "Grady?"

"You're mine, Eden. No more pulling back for me. No changing your mind for you. We do this now, you're with me."

She whimpered, her fingers digging into my sides as she pulled me closer. "I -- I d-don't want anyone else, Grady," she whispered. "I never did."

"You want to do that cam thing, you do it with me. Ain't gonna lie and say I'm good with it, but if it's something you need to do, I'll be the one with you. Not Iron or any of those other bastards. You get me."

"I never want anyone but you Grady," she cried. "No one."

"Good, baby. That's good. 'Cause I'm keepin' you until I die."

Then I sank into her. She wrapped her legs around me and pulled me to her tightly, clinging to me as I moved inside her.

"That's it," I praised, kissing the corner of her mouth, her cheek, her ear. "Take from me what you want. I'll always give you whatever your body desires."

"Grady!" She threw back her head and screamed as I thrust into her. Her pussy contracted around me, making me nearly mindless with the need to come deep inside her. The only thing that helped me hold on was the need to make this last for her. I wanted her to be completely satisfied in a way she never had before. If that meant I was uncomfortable, I could manage. Anything for Eden. She deserved more than I could ever give her, but I'd give her this.

"That's it. You're so beautiful, Eden." I squeezed her to me once before rolling with her so she was on top of me. "You need more?"

"I'll always need more of you, Grady," she whispered. "So good... so fucking good!"

"Yeah, baby. It is. Goddamned fuckin' good." Eden shivered in my arms as I whispered in her ear. Her hips moved in a wicked shimmy over me, keeping us both on the very edge.

I unwrapped my arms and urged her to sit up, stroking my hands up and down her thighs, then up her body to cup her luscious, beautiful, perfect tits. I brushed my thumbs over her nipples before taking them between my fingers and tugging. Her torso rippled with muscle as she moved on me, sliding her pussy up and down my cock in a sensual glide.

The moment she needed more, needed my dominance, I sat up, once again wrapping my arms around her. Eden wrapped her arms around my neck, finding my lips with hers. I laid her back, keeping her thighs open and adjusting my grip on her hips before beginning a hard, driving rhythm.

From my position above her, on my knees, I got a wonderful view of my cock pounding into her. Eden looked from where our bodies joined, to my face and back. Her hair fanned out on the bed all around her, making her look like a wild creature in my arms. Her breath exploded out of her every time my cock surged into her. Her lips were parted, her eyes glazed. She looked like a beautiful nymph, enjoying her pleasure.

When her eyes widened just that little bit, I lay back on top of her, wrapping her up tight in my arms. Her small body was almost completely enveloped by my larger one, and I wanted to shout with the rightness of it. I was made to protect this woman. To pleasure her.

To love her.

"Come with me, Eden," I gasped out. "Your little body is making me come!"

"All mine," she gasped out. "You're all mine!"

"Yeah, baby. Now come for me. Do it!"

She sucked in a breath, her arms tightening around me, and screamed my name. When her pussy contracted around me, it was over. I gave my own brutal yell, bellowing to the ceiling as I came deep inside Eden.

Once the pleasure ebbed inside me, I collapsed on top of Eden. She clung sweetly to me, still trembling.

"You good, baby?"

"Grady," she sighed. "My God…"

"I know." I stroked her face, urging her to look at me when her eyelids drooped. "Look at me for just a moment. Then I'll clean us up and you can sleep." She nodded and met my gaze. There was hesitation in her gaze, almost fear. I suppose I deserved that after the way I'd treated her. "Don't be afraid, baby. I'm not gonna be an asshole again. I swear." That got a little giggle from her and cleared at least some of the shadows from her eyes.

"What is it?" She asked the question with a little trepidation, but I could see she wanted to believe that I wasn't going to hurt her again. That made pain slice through my heart. That anyone could hurt this woman was unthinkable. That it had been me who'd actually done it was inexcusable.

"I need to know we're good, baby. There's a lot happening behind the scenes with your stalker, and I'm going to have to go hunting soon. I need to know you understand that I mean what I say. You're it for me. I'm not leaving you, and I won't hurt you like I've been doing." I winced as I tried to finish, not knowing how. "I need to know you're OK with our age differences. Because I'll be just as bad as your stalker if you leave me. I'm not sure I have it in me to let someone else have you."

"I never said you had to, Grady. Our age difference has never bothered me. It was you who was hung up on that." She blinked slowly, her eyelids obviously heavy. I stroked her face gently, needing to touch her.

"I know. It just never hurts to make sure."

I got up and went to the bathroom for a warm, wet cloth. I cleaned myself before bringing a clean cloth to cleanse Eden. Her eyes were closed, her breathing even. She mumbled in her sleep as I washed her, so I made it brief, wanting to hold her while she slept. Once done, I tossed the cloth in the general direction of the bathroom and slid into bed beside her. Pulling her securely into my arms, I covered us before settling myself. It wasn't long before I drifted off with my Eden. My haven.

My love.

Chapter Six

Grady

I'd dozed off soon after settling with Eden, but woke soon after, my mind too full to rest completely. The full impact of what had happened hit me hard. I was taking this at face value. Really, there was no other option. If she changed her mind I'd have to work harder, but I couldn't lose her. Ever. I felt like a pussy, but my heart was filled with Eden, and I couldn't lose her. I made it through Elizabeth's death -- and it was touch and go for a while -- but Eden had gotten under my skin good. I'd thought before how the dynamic was different this time, and it was. Only I wasn't sure I was the dominant in this relationship. The girl could fucking rule me if she chose.

"Mmmm..." Eden stretched her lithe body, scooting closer to me. She was already half draped over my body, her thigh over my hips, her head on my shoulder, and her fingers digging into my side where she clung so sweetly. "Grady?"

"I'm here, baby." I stroked her back in lazy up-and-down grazes of my fingers. She sounded sleepy, like she was only half awake.

"Was afraid you'd blaze like last time."

I sighed. "Yeah, baby. Never again. I need to leave, I'll wake you and tell you. And I will always come back for you."

She was quiet for a long time. I thought she'd dozed back off, but she must have been thinking just like I was.

"Grady?

"Yeah."

"I can't lose you again. I can't go through the cold shoulder again." Her voice hitched a little, and I realized she was hurt. Really hurt.

"This is how you felt the last time. Wasn't it? When I brushed you off after we had sex in the bed and breakfast on our way here. When I ate your sweet pussy in the truck on the side of the road, then insulted you. I made you cry. Didn't I." It wasn't a question. I just needed the confirmation.

She shrugged. "Does it really matter? I just need you to know I can't go through it again. I can take a lot of things, Grady, but not your rejection of me."

"It matters to me, Eden." I kissed her temple and shifted her so she was fully on top of me. Once I had her settled, I pulled her down for a lingering kiss. She responded beautifully, relaxing against me and letting me kiss her to my heart's content. The little whimpers coming from her warmed my heart.

I ended the kiss and rubbed my face against hers, loving the closeness. Then I sighed. "When we were on the way here, I know I made you cry. I said…" I closed my eyes and winced. "I said unforgivable things to you, Eden. Fuckin' unforgivable."

She met my gaze with her vulnerable one. "What?"

"You are a beautiful, passionate, giving woman, Eden. You gave yourself to me without reservation from the first day I saw you. When we made love, you gave everything you had to the moment. With me. And I just… threw it in your face. I took all that passion and tried to shame you with it."

"Stop," she whispered. "Just stop, Grady."

"No. I'll never stop, Eden. You are… *everything*. Everything in my life that is good comes from you and Charlotte. I need you in my life. Forever. If you'll give me the chance, I'll spend the rest of my fuckin' life making it all up to you." One tear tracked down her cheek, and her lips parted in surprise, but she stayed still.

For a long time we stared at each other. Silent tears tracked down her face. First that one. Then more. Her lips quivered before she raised that stubborn chin of hers in that way that turned me one so fucking much. She sat up, her shoulders back, those glorious tits of hers beckoning me to touch, but I didn't dare. Then she reached behind her and guided my cock into her entrance and sat back. A groan was torn from my chest, and I had to grip her hips tightly to keep her from moving. 'Cause, if she moved, I was coming. No question.

"Talk to me, baby," I begged, needing her to tell me what she was thinking. "I'll do anything to make this right."

"Why did you say those things to me?" There seemed to be two different things happening at the same time. Eden wanted answers, but she was also moving on me like she intended to make me lose my fucking mind.

"I was trying to drive you away. I knew I could never be what you needed, and you weren't taking the hint." I wanted to leave it there, but I couldn't. After what I'd put her through, Eden deserved the whole truth. "Also, I was trying to protect myself. I wanted you so Goddamned bad I was afraid if I gave you a chance, you'd take my heart and I'd never be the same person." I sighed. "Look. I'm ex-special forces. Force Recon. I'm still in good shape, thanks to my career. I've always tried to be strong in body and mind, but I'm still forty-three. Eventually you'll want someone younger. I'd hoped that you'd find someone else. Someone closer to your age who could love you like you deserved."

"Then you ran off anyone who looked my way," she said, smiling for the first time.

"Yeah. I ran off anyone who looked your way. And I knew I'd continue to run the fuckers off 'cause you're mine."

"Little confused there, huh?"

"I was," I said, rubbing my hands up her thighs to her hips and back. "Not anymore. It's you for me, Eden. I've already had one woman I loved more than life and lost her to cancer. I never once even thought about wanting another woman. I had my daughter to take care of and knew I'd never have time for another person that close to me. Then I saw you. I was so worried about Charlotte I couldn't appreciate the beauty you were, but it didn't take long for me to become obsessed with you. Just like your fuckin' stalker."

Immediately, she lay down on top of me, stopping the movements of her hips. "You listen to me, Lawdawg," she said. I couldn't help the wince.

"Lawdawg? Really, Eden?"

"Not the point of this conversation, but yeah. Lawdawg. You are nothing like that stupid stalker. You're my choice. My man. I don't want anyone younger. I don't want someone prettier or sweeter, or who expects me to be the perfect lady. You're it for me. I'm it for you. We'll be perfect together, Grady. Me and you."

"We good, then? Because I don't want you thinkin' about what a dumbass bastard I am. I'll never forget what I did, and I'll spend the rest of my life making it up to you, but I don't want you afraid it's gonna happen again."

"Ain't sayin' I won't ever bring it up, especially when I want something, but I'll trust that you've learned from your mistakes. Just remember. Next time it happens, I'm taking it to Samson. He'll get to decide your punishment."

"Yeah," I grinned. "He'd kill me, and I'd stand there and let him."

"No, you won't," she said decisively. "You'll fight because you know I still need you. No matter what. But just remember I can and will make your life miserable."

"You'll never have to, baby." I kissed her again, framing her face in my hands.

Then she proceeded to blow my mind, taking me higher than we'd been together so far. Every time I thought I'd reached the pinnacle of pleasure with her, the bar got fucking smashed. I was helpless in her arms, in her body. And there was never a place I wanted to be more.

Afterward, we lay spent, coated in sweat. She was still sprawled on top of me. My cock was still semi-hard and firmly inside her. My cum leaked over my balls where it dripped out of Eden, but I had never been more comfortable and content.

We lay there together just like that. I managed to pull the covers over us and wrapped my arms around Eden. She was my woman. My love. My heart and soul. To me it sounded corny, but I remember enough of what Elizabeth taught me about love to know it was love I felt for Eden. I thought I'd struggle more with this because Elizabeth had been such a big part of my life, but one of the last things she said to me was that she wanted me happy. I knew she'd be good with my relationship with Eden. I just needed to make sure Charlotte was good, too.

* * *

I was sound asleep when I heard Grady's phone buzz on the nightstand beside us. I lay with my head on his chest. The steady beating of his heart had lulled me to sleep after our talk. There were still things we needed to discuss, but all in all, I felt secure in our relationship now. The mere fact that he realized how much he'd hurt me and had owned up to it had meant more than he could possibly imagine. But when that phone buzzed, I got a sick feeling in my gut. Was this when he left me?

Grady stirred, groaning as he reached for the little fucker and read the text. It wasn't long after he read the text his phone rang.

"Yeah. Grady." There was a long silence while whoever called talked. Grady was silent until the end. "I'll be there." Then he hung up.

He kissed the top of my head. When he laid the phone back on the nightstand, he wrapped his arms around me tightly and didn't move for long seconds. Then he seemed to make a decision. Grady pulled me more fully on top of him before rolling us, so he was settled comfortably between my legs.

Stroking my hair away from my face, he looked down into my eyes. "Did I tell you how beautiful you are, baby?"

"Not like I'd mind hearing it again," I said, grinning up at him.

"You're so fuckin' beautiful it hurts to look at you sometimes," he whispered. Then he kissed me until I was begging him to fuck me. And, honestly, it didn't take much. The man was the sexiest guy I'd ever seen and the most giving lover I'd ever had.

Instead of keeping me on the edge like he liked

to do, Grady brought me up high and fast, pushing me
from one orgasm into another until he found his own
completion with a brutal shout. I clung to him, just
riding it out. Letting him have me however he needed
me. Something was getting ready to happen, and I
dreaded each moment knowing it would end this time
we had together. While I was eager for the next phase
of our life, I worried he might be underestimating this
stalker simply because the guy hadn't shown his face.

As he continued to kiss me softly, he murmured.
"I gotta go, baby. Samson said they've found your
stalker and are ready to make their move. It's time to
go hunting."

"Can't you let Bones take care of it? They work
well together. Introducing a new person into the mix
might not be such a good thing. You could, I don't
know, stay here. Make sure the compound is secure."
The second I said it, I wished I could take it back. Not
because I didn't mean it, but because I knew Grady
would think I didn't believe he could handle himself. I
couldn't meet his gaze but could practically feel his
stare burning into me.

Then his fingers stroked my chin gently, tipping
my face up to his. He leaned in and kissed me gently,
pulling back and giving me a cocky grin. "You worried
about me?"

"Of course, I'm worried about you," I snapped.
His cock was still firmly inside me, and my hands
tightened on his hips, my fingers digging into his skin.
"This guy worries me!"

"I know, baby." He kissed my nose, still stroking
my hair in a soothing rub. "That's why I'm going out
there to make sure we get him. I don't want to leave
anything out there to chance."

"You can't just kill the guy. He's not done

anything other than make himself a pain in my ass."

"Not sure of the end result. We are keeping an open mind. Guy might just need to be scared straight. As VP of Black Reign and president of Bones, that decision will be left to Samson and Cain."

That took me off guard. "You're not making that decision?"

He smirked. "Not unless I don't agree with their decision."

I punched him in the shoulder. "You're gonna get yourself in trouble."

Grady kissed me again. "Well, if anything is worth it, it's you, baby." He kissed me once more before getting out of bed and getting dressed.

"Stay in the compound. I'll be in touch and will let you know the second everything is over."

"Promise me you're coming back?"

"Absolutely, baby. Nothing will ever keep me away from you again." Once he was dressed, he opened his arms to me. "Come here."

I ran to his arms and clung. Those strong arms of his felt so good, and I didn't want to let go. All too soon, though, Grady pulled back, framing my face with those big hands of his.

"Only got one more thing to say to you before I go. And I want you to really listen to me."

"What is it?"

He kissed me tenderly before putting his forehead to mine. "I love you, Eden. With all my heart I love you."

To my utter horror, I burst into tears, throwing myself into his arms and clinging tightly to him. Grady just let me cry it out, holding me and murmuring to me soothingly. I'd known love all my life. After my parents died, Samson had been as fierce a protector as ever there could have been. But, though I knew how much he loved and cared for me, Samson wasn't the overly affectionate type. He probably was with Lottie, but as a rule, he was pretty stoic.

"That's the first time in a long time anyone's told me that." I hated admitting it to Grady because I didn't want him to think I was pathetic, but I wanted him to know the words meant so much to me. "I love you, too."

He frowned. "Samson doesn't tell you?"

I rolled my eyes even as I wiped them with my hand. "Samson loves me. He's just not the affectionate type. Plus, he tried to avoid me unless he knew something was wrong. Said he didn't want to kill any of his brothers for touching me."

"I get that." Grady chuckled. "That's something else I'll make sure you get a lot of." He kissed me once more. "Now. I've got to go. Remember," he said, giving me a pointed look. "Stay in the compound. I promise I'll be in touch."

* * *

Eden

When Grady left me this morning to go out with the rest of Bones to find my stalker, I thought I could handle it. But after hours of wandering around the clubhouse, talking with Lottie, and sitting in my room, I knew this wasn't going to work for me. I was so nervous I couldn't sit still. Every time I tried to eat, I was afraid I'd puke.

"You know they'll be fine. Right?" Angel, Cain's ol' lady, had sidled up to me at the bar in the common room. She gave me a serene smile. "Cain wouldn't let them do this if he wasn't confident he could get them out."

"I guess he'd have to be pretty good at his job to own a successful security company."

"Yes. Cain is very protective by nature. He's hard on the guys when they're preparing for an operation, but it's for everyone's safety. He said he lost too many friends when he was in the Corps to lose more now that he was out."

"I can't help but worry." I tried to smile at her, but I knew my lips trembled. "I just found him. I don't want to lose him."

"It'll be OK. Maybe if you had a drink, then lie down. Has he texted you?"

"Yes. Several times." I smiled again, but a tear spilled and dripped down my cheek. "He tells me he loves me every time he texts."

"I'm so happy for you," Angel said, her smile as genuine as her words. "If he's anything like Cain, he's a good man. Cain said they served together in the Corps."

I nodded. "That's the reason Grady brought me here. He said he could trust Cain to keep me safe here until they could ferret out my stalker."

"Well, I'm glad Grady thought to bring you here." She reached out and took my hand. "The two of you are welcome here any time."

"Thank you." I looked around. "Grady said I might be able to check up on them through Data? Said he was their tech guy, and that he could keep me informed if I need an update. Said not to text him for the next few hours. Do you know where I could find Data?"

"Absolutely! Come with me."

Angel took me to an office with a wall full of monitors. It reminded me of the tech room in crime TV shows. Wall-to-wall monitors with a big screen in the center. Only… smaller. In the center of it all sat a man in his early to mid-forties and a woman in her mid- to late-twenties. Both seemed intent on their screens, talking to one another in hushed tones.

Angel touched the man on the shoulder. "Grady's woman is behind you, Data," she said softly.

The girl sitting beside Data turned and waved brightly at me. "I'm Suzie," she whispered. "Zora's in the other room working on actually tracking the guy, but you can ask me any questions you have. Just give me a minute. They're in a tricky spot." I nodded my understanding. Angel patted me on the shoulder before leaving.

There were several conversations going on over the speakers. I strained but couldn't hear Grady's voice among all the others. It seemed that I was hearing the conversations of more than one team in the field and one at the actual site where they expected to confront my stalker. Watching the monitors, I realized it was the Boneyard I was looking at from so many different angles. Both inside and out. Was this thing taking place there?

"Suzie," I whispered. "Is that the Boneyard? The club's bar?"

She didn't say anything but turned her head slightly and nodded at me. I sat as still as I could, trying not to be a distraction to the two people at the control panel. It looked like they were having to pay attention to every conversation going on around them. Once or twice, Data spoke to the teams, giving them sets of numbers I thought were probably times and distance. All I knew was I was getting more and more nervous the longer this went on. My heart felt like it was going to pound out of my chest.

Then I saw him. Grady. He sat at the bar looking

every bit as relaxed as if he were just another patron with nothing amiss. There were other men in the bar, but I saw only Grady. Sitting there sipping a beer. He was taking all the risks while I was sitting here in a safe little cocoon when this was my problem. I'd been the one to attract a stalker. It was me who should be responsible for all this shit. Not Grady and his friends.

Quietly, so as not to disturb Data and Suzie, I slipped out of the office and stood outside for long moments. What did I do now? Stay here? Let everyone around me take the risks while I sat safe in my little cocoon?

I went to the door and studied the surrounding property. There were prospects and patched members everywhere, obviously in a defensive stance. They'd locked the compound down tight.

"What's up?" Vanya, one of the club girls, gave me the once-over.

"Nothing. I just need to get scarce." Wasn't her business, and I didn't want everyone in the Goddamned place knowing I wanted off the property.

"Well, good luck with that. They've got the place locked down like Fort Knox. No one in or out."

Knowing that little bit helped, because I knew they'd have all the obvious places covered. So I had to find the not-so-obvious places. Having spent the better part of my life in one of the most secure compounds in existence, I was good at finding ways out. This time would be no exception.

"How many guys they got looking after the place?" I asked the woman. "I mean, I thought most were out helping Grady with something."

"First of all," Vanya said with a scowl, "It's Grady helping Bones. And yeah. They took most of the guys with them. But there are twelve prospects here and another five patched members to guard the place. All of them work for ExFil so they ain't no slouches."

So, seventeen men. I just had to account for all of them and I'd have my way out. I couldn't help but grin as I slipped through the one break in the wall they hadn't covered. It was probably a back path for bikes only, though it was only a guess. Black Reign didn't have anything like it. Just a door in the back of the compound next to a wooded area. So I got through and took the woods out until I came to the road. From there, I knew how to get to the Boneyard.

Getting to the bar took me another hour since I was on foot and sticking to the woods. Once there, I studied the place for a bit. It looked like business as usual. Nothing indicated there was anything out of the ordinary. There might not have been as many bikes out front as there had been the other times I'd been there, but it was Wednesday. There probably weren't as many patrons in the middle of the week.

I approached from the back instead of the front since I'd come out of the woods. There was a door at the side, but it was guarded. The guy didn't appear too interested in his job, which I was sure Cain wouldn't be too happy about but fuck him. I wanted in, so the lax security was in my best interest. I waited until the guard wandered around the front of the building -- probably to see if anyone was near the front. When he stopped at the corner and lit a cigarette, I let myself in quietly. The door was near the restroom, off the main room. I could hear men's voices and the music from the jukebox, but the music was too loud to make out what they were saying from this distance.

When I stepped into the main room, I saw several of the Bones men. At the bar was Grady. His face was grim and focused on a man I didn't know. He looked rather out of place for a biker bar, but I understood they had a diverse clientele. Grady wasn't sociable on the best of days. Maybe he just didn't like the looks of the guy.

Then the guy's gaze drifted my way, and he looked spooked. Like a trapped animal surrounded by wolves. His eyes widened. He was just a few feet away.

Next thing I know, he lunged for me and pulled me in front of him. The steel of a gun barrel pressed against my temple, and he pulled back the hammer.

Chapter Seven

Grady

The bastard's name was Mace Carter. He was a fucking used car salesman for Christ's sake! Guy had seen Eden's show and fixated on her. Once he got the balls to run off her more vocal followers, he got it in his head he could have Eden. Well, that wasn't fucking happening.

"You got two choices, man," Cain said. "You leave, or I give you to Lawdawg there."

"But I want her. My pretty little Candy. She should change her real name to Candy."

The man wasn't in his right mind. That much was easy to tell.

"This ain't gonna go down good," Data said, his voice soft in the earwig he'd given us all. "Man's whacked out." It certainly did look like he was high.

"How we gonna talk him down?" Bohannon muttered from his place next to me. "He's high as a fuckin' kite."

"Probably had to be to make this kind of a move. Not the type to make a run for a woman he's infatuated with under normal circumstances."

"He made it from Florida to here," I muttered. "Had plenty of time to change his mind or sober up."

"Yeah," Bohannon said. "As long as he uses, he'll always come back to her. Brother," Bohannon gave me a hard look. "Guy's gonna always be a shadow over her."

I looked from Bohannan back to the little fuck. "No." 'Cause, no matter what Cain wanted, this guy was fuckin' dead. Bohannon knew it, too. He didn't agree with me, but I could see he accepted it. Cain would probably kick my ass. Or try. But this guy wasn't living past tonight.

Movement caught my eye. No one was supposed to be in that area. Fucking prospect was supposed to be watching the fucking door. Which was when Carter moved. He lunged toward the hallway. A woman's shriek followed. Next thing I knew, Carter had Eden, his arm around her front while he hunkered down behind her. A gun to her temple.

"Woah, there," Deadeye said from across the room. "Let's not do anything rash."

Sweat beaded Carter's face. Adrenaline was flooding his bloodstream. That, combined with whatever drug he was on, would not be a good combination. I already had one hand on my gun, ready to pull it at the first opportunity.

"Stop and think about what you're doing, young man." From behind the bar, Pops tried to calm the fucker. Carter's gaze darted between Pops and Deadeye, the two speaking. It was why they spoke. To divert attention from Bohannon and Cain. And me.

My eyes locked with Eden's. She was startled and frightened, knowing all too well the danger she was in. My heart lurched and sped up. I wanted to charge the bastard, but his fuckin' gun was cocked and ready. One jerk of his finger would kill Eden.

"Eden," I snapped. "Eyes on me. Don't look away."

"Grady," she whispered, her lips trembling. Her hands were at her sides, but trembling. Her right hand shook and rubbed nervously up and down her jeans-clad legs.

"I don't wanna do this, man," Carter said, tears starting to flow. "I love her, don't you see that?"

"Let her go, Carter," Pops said. "If you love her, let her go."

Carter shook his head several times, strongly. "No. If I can't have her, no one will." He leaned into Eden, his eyes crazy. Inhaling, he rubbed his face against hers. Eden cringed but stayed perfectly still. It took every ounce of discipline I had to not pull my gun. I had to wait until the right time. He'd let up his guard for a split second before he pulled the trigger. He'd hesitate just that little bit, because he really didn't want to kill Eden. I was pretty sure the fucker knew he was dead and wanted to take Eden with him. I'd seen it more than once. But who the fuck really knew? I was going on blind instinct.

I took a breath.

"Goodbye, Eden," Carter whispered by her ear. "We'll be together soon."

He closed his eyes as he pulled the trigger.

Three things happened on top of each other. First, Eden gave a fierce yell and brought her hand down on Carter's thigh. Carter's gun went off a split second after. Three more guns went off almost simultaneously, exploding Carter's head.

Eden dropped to the floor. There was fucking blood and brains and bone every fucking where.

"Eden!" I roared her name, my gaze glued on her. My vision tunneled until I saw only Eden. Her arms were above her head where she lay on the floor. "Eden!"

I was on her in an instant, shoving her arms away from her head, dreading to see but needing to all the same. I expected to see a mass of blood and hair before I turned her over to stare into lifeless eyes. My Eden.

"Grady," she whimpered before pulling away and dragging herself to her feet. She didn't let me help her but stood on her own. Which just pissed me the fuck off. I grabbed her arm and yanked her into my arms, hugging her so tightly she gasped for breath.

"Don't you ever fuckin' stay where you're fuckin' put?" I know I sounded harsh and angry as fuck. I *was* angry. But I was more scared than angry. Which pissed me off even more. "Goddamn it, Eden!"

"Grady, let me go. I can't breathe." Her strained voice was the only thing that let me loosen up on her, though not by much. I wanted to wrap her up forever to keep her safe.

Samson was next to her, his hands gripping her shoulders, trying to pry her from my arms. I looked up at the big man and bared my teeth. "Mine!"

"Hey. No one said she wasn't yours. But you gotta loosen your hold on her, brother." Somewhere inside, I knew Samson was right, but I couldn't make myself. I'd nearly lost her. Just like I'd lost Elizabeth. The beast inside me was still raging with fear and grief even though I was holding Eden and she was safe.

"Take a couple breaths, Grady. She's good." That was Bohannon.

"You need to take her out of here so we can clean up the fuckin' mess," Cain said. His voice was gruff, but soft. "Take her home, brother."

I scooped Eden up in my arms. Thankfully, she wrapped her slim arms around my neck and clung, burying her face in my neck. Her slight body trembled, sweat making her shirt stick to her body. I could smell her fear, but she refused to cry. Not here with everyone witnessing. In that moment, not only was Eden my woman, she became my hero. Because it was the same moment I realized tears were streaking down my fucking face like a waterfall.

"It's all right," she whispered. "I'm all right."

"Damned straight you are," I growled. "When

we get back to the fucking house, imma beat your ass so hard you won't sit down for a fuckin' month!"

"I know," she said. "I know. I'm so sorry, Grady! I just didn't want you to face this guy alone."

"I wasn't alone, Eden! Fuck! I had fuckin' Bones with me! Cain! Samson! The computer geeks!" I was yelling at her at the same time I held her close. "We had it under control!"

"I know," she kept repeating. "I know, I know."

"Fuck!" I took a deep breath, inhaling the fresh spring air. She was fine. She was with me. "You're fine, baby," I said out loud. "You're fine. I've got you."

"I've got you, too, Grady. I've got you too."

* * *

Eden

Once we were back at the clubhouse, Grady did, indeed, paddle my ass but good. I wasn't sure I'd be able to sit down for the foreseeable future, but it had turned me on like nothing else. Grady had looked at me like I'd grown a second head, then fucked me into oblivion. It was a long time before we got out of bed after that round.

The party Bones threw the next night was one for the ages. Three clubs were in attendance. Bones, Salvation's Bane, and Black Reign. Cain had even invited El Diablo. Of course, the Reign president had jumped at the chance to spend time with his daughter, Magenta. Sword, her man, was more than a little disgruntled, but Magenta seemed to be having a wonderful time talking with her father, and Grady had to ride Cain about it.

"Growin' soft in your old age?"

"Nah. That was all Angel. She insisted, and I have a hard time denying her anything."

"I'd rag you for being pussy whipped, but I'm right there with you."

"Grady!" He kissed my temple where he stood with his arm solidly around me. The man loved staking his claim, and I loved it when he did.

I saw Iron across the room. He gave Grady a salute as he wrapped his arm around the shoulders of a woman drinking a beer. Grady nodded at the other man. Iron's way of telling Grady he had nothing to fear from him.

"Where's Charlotte?" I hadn't seen her yet, but I knew Samson would send for her when the other Black Reign members headed this way. Sure enough, she called out from the doorway where she and the Black Reign ol' ladies strolled through the door, looking for their men.

"Daddy!" She ran to Grady, throwing her arms around him and kissing his cheek. "I was so worried!" Immediately, she turned to me and hugged me just as fiercely. "Why didn't you call when things got bad?"

I ducked her head and shrugged. "I was scared. In retrospect, it might have been better if I had called you. It would have saved your dad a huge scare and me a sore ass."

Charlotte tilted her head. "What?"

Eden snorted. "He spanked me."

"Oh... OH! Well, fuck me raw!" She and Eden burst out laughing.

When our merriment simmered, Grady gently turned Charlotte to face him. "Baby. Are you good with this? With me and Eden?"

She gave him a warm smile. "Daddy, all I've ever wanted was for you to be happy. If Eden makes you happy, then keep her. Besides, there is no other woman in this world I'd rather have as a stepmom." She turned to me and grinned.

"You're my sister," I said. Yeah. I could see us getting into all kinds of mischief together. Then we hugged again. "You take care of my big brother."

"You take care of my dad."

El Diablo approached us, a welcoming smile on his face. "Grady. So glad to see you." The other man stuck out his hand, taking Grady's in a firm grip. "You remember my lovely wife, Jezebel."

The dark headed woman waved. "Are you guys coming back to Florida?" She looked almost hopeful when her gaze landed on Lottie and Eden. "I like having the other ol' ladies around. Helps me keep this one in line if he knows I've got cohorts. There's power in numbers," she said with a grin.

Grady looked at me. I wanted to go back to Lake Worth. To Black Reign. But I wasn't sure what Grady wanted. He was a sheriff in another county. It wasn't far, but still.

"We haven't discussed it," he said. Then looked down at me. "But I don't imagine we'll ever be too far. That's Eden's home and family."

El Diablo leaned close. "You know, we could use you as a brother in Black Reign. Having law enforcement on hand can sometimes come in handy."

"Really?" Grady's eyebrows rose. "I'd've thought you'd want to keep me as far away from the club as possible."

"Nonsense," El Diablo waved his hand, dismissing Grady's concern. "You've proven to be a valuable asset. Besides, I'd never expect you to be a part of anything to go against your oath of office. I'd only expect you to mete out justice where you saw fit. And you'd have the full weight of the club behind you. Nothing you've not already done, and never indiscriminately."

I could see the wheels turning in Grady's mind. Weighing all the pros and cons. "I can see where my presence could be beneficial at times. Just as long as you understand there will be times I might disagree with you and go my own way."

El Diablo chuckled. "That pretty much sums up every man in Black Reign. So what do you say?"

Grady held out for a heartbeat, then grinned, extending his hand to El Diablo again. "I think I can handle that. But, for the record, I ain't gonna be no prospect."

"Nor would I expect you to. You've already proven yourself with the ruthlessness you showed in getting your daughter back and protecting our precious Eden. That's all I want or expect."

"Then you have my loyalty."

"You and Rycks can get together on how you want to proceed. He does so love rescuing those in need."

"That, I'd be happy to do."

"A toast, then!" El Diablo raised his beer and invited everyone else to do the same. "To the newest patched member of Black Reign!" Everyone shouted and congratulated Grady. Jezebel presented him with two vests. One was his, with the Black Reign colors on the back, the other was a property vest with "Property of" on the top rocker and "Lawdawg" on the bottom rocker. I had to stifle my giggle when Grady scowled.

"Lawdawg? Really?"

El Diablo just smiled. "Samson said it suited you. I agree."

"Fuckers," Grady muttered. Everyone else laughed even as they clapped Grady on the back, welcoming him into Black Reign.

Cain shook his hand, shaking his head as he did. "I guess that's one more tie Black Reign has with Bones."

Grady shrugged. "It is what it is, brother. Maybe you should consider moving Reign up to sister club instead of rival club."

"Like I have a fuckin' choice. You're not Bones, but you've been my brother as long as anyone in Bones. With Magenta and Stunner, I suppose we're tied as tightly as they come. Still don't mean I trust El Diablo."

"Ah, now, Cain," El Diablo said, a mock look of hurt on his face. "Don't be so mean. I've mellowed since I found my daughter and married my sweet Jezebel. We can be friends."

"Right," Cain said with a wry smile. "I'll just be over here hiding all my ExFil contacts." There was a time when El Diablo eyed Bones greedily for the resource Cain's paramilitary security company provided. Stunner had been sent to scout the territory when, in reality, Stunner had only wanted to make sure the three children he'd sent Bones's way were taken care of. It had been a point of contention between him and Cain when Cain found out, but they'd since reconciled. Stunner was also happily married to Suzie, Cain's daughter, with the blessing of both Cain and Angel.

"Fear not! I've decided to offer you my services in the area of ExFil," El Diablo said. "Not only can I bring you solid contacts, but I can offer training in both surveillance and enhanced interrogation. Not to mention offer you another team of elite soldiers to work with. I promised last Christmas I'd help. Here I am."

"Uh-huh," Cain glanced at Grady. I had to

wonder what El Diablo's game was, but honestly, no one ever knew what the other man wanted.

"Just think about it. The offer is sincere and with no strings. I only want strength in numbers. Our three clubs could be the strongest in the southeastern part of the country. We'd be able to clean up certain aspects of other clubs' businesses and make life better for the average person. All for the greater good, you understand."

"You're so full of shit." Cain chuckled. "But I will give it serious thought."

"That's all I ask," El Diablo said. "Now. I fully intend to see to it my lovely wife enjoys herself. If you will all excuse me." El Diablo leaned in and kissed Jezebel gently. The other woman smiled before wrapping her arms around him. He just picked her up and carried her over to a corner couch and sat her on his lap.

"Looks like a happy couple," Grady commented.

"Yeah," Samson said, handing Grady another beer. "He's almost like a different man now that he has Jezebel. She takes the edge off." He grinned. "Good to have you in the group, Lawdawg."

Grady groaned. "When we get home, remind me to spank your ass again, Eden."

"Me? What the hell'd I do?" I laughed, knowing full well I was the first person to call him Lawdawg.

"You know exactly what you fuckin' did." Grady sounded disgruntled, but his face was relaxed, a smile hovering just beyond his lips.

"Tell you what. If you promise to do what you did to me after you spanked me before, I'll remind you when we get home."

That got laughs in our circle of friends.

I looked up at Grady. My man. "You know I love

you, right?"

He smiled back down at me, leaning in for a soft kiss. "Yeah, baby. I know. I love you, too. So fuckin' much."

"Come dance with me," I said, already leading him to the middle of the room where other couples swayed to some power ballad I didn't pay attention to. I just wanted to hold my man close for a while. I knew he wanted to hold me too. We could have left the party to go to our room, but I think we both needed the comfort of being surrounded by friends.

So we danced among the camaraderie. We relished the time together.

And we loved each other every fucking second.

From now to eternity.

Marteeka Karland

Erotic romance author by night, emergency room tech/clerk by day, Marteeka Karland works really hard to drive everyone in her life completely and totally nuts. She has been creating stories from her warped imagination since she was in the third grade. Her love of writing blossomed throughout her teenage years until it developed into the totally unorthodox and irreverent style her English teachers tried so hard to rid her of.

Marteeka at Changeling: changelingpress.com/marteeka-karland-a-39

Changeling Press E-Books

More Sci-Fi, Fantasy, Paranormal, and BDSM adventures available in e-book format for immediate download at ChangelingPress.com -- Werewolves, Vampires, Dragons, Shapeshifters and more -- Erotic Tales from the edge of your imagination.

What are E-Books?

E-books, or electronic books, are books designed to be read in digital format -- on your desktop or laptop computer, notebook, tablet, Smart Phone, or any electronic e-book reader.

Where can I get Changeling Press E-Books?

Changeling Press e-books are available at ChangelingPress.com, Amazon, Apple Books, Barnes & Noble, and Kobo/Walmart.

ChangelingPress.com